YOU

WATCH

TURN

YOUR

TO

BACK

DIE

SUE WALLMAN

Scholastic Children's Books
An imprint of Scholastic Ltd
Euston House, 24 Eversholt Street, London, NW1 1DB, UK
Registered office: Westfield Road, Southam, Warwickshire, CV47 0RA
SCHOLASTIC and associated logos are trademarks and/or
registered trademarks of Scholastic Inc.

First published in the UK by Scholastic Ltd, 2018

ISBN 978 1407 18158 5

A CIP catalogue record for this book
is available from the British Library.

Printed by CPI Group (UK) Ltd, Croydon, CR0 4YY
Papers used by Scholastic Children's Books are made
from wood grown in sustainable forests.

1 3 5 7 9 10 8 6 4 2

www.scholastic.co.uk

For Phoebe, Maia and Sophie xxx

ONE

The back seat of the car is my kingdom. Travel duvet, phone, headphones, snacks, easy-to-access make-up bag to make myself look presentable ten minutes before arrival. Not even the presence of revision books, hastily stuffed into my bag by Mum, can dampen my mood. I pop a tab of chewing gum into my mouth, crunching down with satisfaction on the minty outer layer. Not long to go until we're there.

I'm wrong about that. It takes ages to reach the midway point, the Spotted Pig pub. It was where we always stopped for lunch when it was Mum and Dad. Now it's Mum and Steve, and Mum drives straight past it without saying anything. She pulls up outside a cafe in a parade of shops off the main road. It turns out to be closed, so we have to buy sandwiches from a petrol station.

We eat the ham and cheese (with unexpected mayonnaise) sandwiches and Pringles in a parking space next to the machine that forces air into car tyres. Steve finds his Guess the Movie Soundtrack app and I'm annoyed to discover my new headphones fail to block the grating sound of him and Mum laughing.

I remind myself that in a couple of days the two of them will be going up north to visit Steve's sister, leaving me at Roeshot House alone with the others. I. Cannot. Wait.

Before we set off again, Mr Eager-To-Please takes the rubbish to the bin. While he's gone, Mum checks her face in the flip-down mirror above the windscreen. She pushes away a flake of mascara from her cheek, and reapplies her lipstick. By the bin, Steve straightens his Christmas jumper. I know what everyone at Roeshot House is going to think about that jumper.

"Mum," I say. "Please don't let Steve share any more of the driving."

She frowns.

"He has a solid driving age of ninety," I say. Leaving aside the fact he owns driving gloves, I concentrate on the main problem: by driving so slowly he's wasting valuable time I could be spending with my cousin Ivy and our lifelong friend Jakob. "I hate being the last ones to arrive."

Mum sighs and looks as if she's about to fire up the Don't-Be-Mean-To Steve script, but she says, "You're right to want to make the most of Roeshot House. I'm not sure I'll be able to afford it next year if the rental price keeps rocketing. And Steve and I aren't even going to be there for two of the nights we're paying for." She sees my face and starts the engine as Steve approaches the car. "I'll do my best but, you know, maybe next year it'll be time for us to do something different."

I'm not sure who the "us" is in that sentence.

I lean forward to the gap in between the front seats. "But we have to come back next year."

"Soon you'll want to go to a New Year party with your friends at home," says Mum. "Things change."

"They already have," I say, leaning back as Steve opens the car door and sits so heavily the car actually wobbles, adding one of his trademark grunty noises. "Everything all right?" he says. He's not the sharpest tool in the shed, but I think even he can sense he's not my favourite person.

I pretend I haven't heard, and Mum says, "Yes, we're fine, thanks. Leah's keen to get there and see Ivy and Jakob."

She makes me sound as if I'm going on a play date. When we were little, Ivy, Jakob and I called ourselves the Three Amigos. It sounds silly now that we're fifteen, but that's still how we think of ourselves.

I can't imagine a time when I'd rather be at a party than at Roeshot House. OK, it sounds supremely unpromising when I tell anyone about it: a week in an old house in the middle of nowhere which has no Wi-Fi or even a phone signal. But somehow it works. The three of us hang out by ourselves most of the time, sometimes also with my little cousin Poppy, Ivy's sister, who's eight, and their dog Baz. The adults are always busy being boring with each other, which works fine for us.

We've lost two dads along the way. My uncle, Ivy and Poppy's dad, died of a heart attack three years ago, and my dad dropped out last year after he left to live with Amber. The Amigos were there for each other both times, not in a weepy arms-round-each-other kind of way, but by escaping to where we'd always been happy, up in the attic. We did our usual things, the predictions, of course, and mad games, like doing laps of the attic without our feet touching the floor, which involved climbing on the bookshelves and leaping from the big desk with the green leather inlay on to the armchair, crawling on top of the chest of drawers, and cheating with the rug for the last bit. There were always new things to do or to talk about. Like the time last year when Jakob produced a load of miniature bottles of alcohol his parents had won ages ago in a raffle and forgotten about. We discovered a taste for Chinese liqueurs and made our own chocolate ones by buying hollow chocolate Father Christmases and injecting the alcohol in with the oral syringe we found in the bathroom alongside an out-of-date bottle of Calpol.

Being an Amigo was about having fun, not dwelling on the crap that had happened in the past year.

My phone pings. A notification appears at the top of

my screen. It's Ivy. *Where are you?* She's placed the text across a selfie of herself, her face indignant, her eyes the same shade of brown as mine. The two of us look more alike as cousins than our mums do as sisters.

I catch a glimpse of grey cloud behind her. She'll be sitting on the wall at the end of the drive for the phone signal. The next shot is of a cow in the field next to Roeshot House. Then another of her with a snowman filter that's given her a carrot nose. *Freezing my arse off. Hurry up and get here.*

I have an excuse, I message back. *It's called Steve. You'll understand when you meet him.*

I watch Steve rub his bald patch absent-mindedly. I begged Mum not to invite him. He won't understand the traditions. He probably won't even appreciate the house. It's a blend of new and old. Every time we arrive we find that Pinhurst Properties has renovated it a little bit more and Mum insists that it was perfectly fine how it was before and it didn't need the wet room installing downstairs, or the new coffee machine. But I like the gradual makeover, the high ceilings and the space. I love the two staircases at different ends of the house, and how there's a cluster of bedrooms for the adults at one end, and another for the Amigos and Poppy at the other. Above all, I love how we can make as much noise in the attic as we like, and as long as we check in for meals nobody minds much what we do.

"Nearly there," says Mum. She turns her head towards Steve, I guess giving him a smile, though I can't see it from where I'm sitting, but I see her hand rest momentarily on his thigh, and wish I hadn't. "Gabs and Elaine can be overbearing, but don't let that bother you. They just like things their way," she says. Mum's right: my auntie Gabs and her best friend from school, Elaine, can be terrifying. I wonder if he's nervous. Mum turns her attention back to the road, and the indicator tick-tocks as she slows down to turn right. "I'd never have believed we'd end up spending every New Year together, the three of us. Gabs and Elaine pretended I didn't exist most of my childhood." She says it as if it's amusing, but I don't find it funny.

We're on the twisty roads now and there's only one bar on my phone left. I circle a porthole in the condensation on my window. The grey-white light is darkening. The frost hasn't thawed all day. Ivy will be back in the house now with the others, keeping warm by the log fire.

We pass the sign to the Holiday Village, the open-all-year-round mobile home park which has an indoor pool where Ivy once organized a competition to see how many floating plasters we could scoop up. It was something like seven, and Auntie Gabs took them to the front reception and got a refund on our entrance fee.

There are still Christmas lights up in the village, and the most ostentatious display is above the Chinese takeaway as usual. Two boys on bikes, leaning against the postbox, stare at our car and I want to tell them that we half-belong here. At least, Mum and I do.

I rush to rub concealer over the spot on my chin, holding my tiny mirror near the window where the light is better, then put on my trainers, but I keep looking up. Seeing Roeshot House for the first time as we turn into the drive is a sight I've never become tired of. The house is imposing and proud, built from beautiful old grey stone, with a circular section of drive outside the big, square porch. The front door is huge and wooden and looks like something out of an old-fashioned Christmas card with its large wreath, made with real foliage and different each year, and with the little lantern-like lights lit up either side of it.

It's around three times the size of our old house, four times the size of our new one. The new house is dull. You can look at it from outside and can pretty much guess the layout inside. Roeshot House promises surprises: corridors and hidden-away rooms, cupboards in unusual places and bathrooms the size of our lounge.

Smoke rises from the chimney into the approaching-dusk sky. There are two cars already parked near the porch. I knew we'd be the last to arrive.

As I step on to the drive, my legs stiff with not having moved for a while, I see a car slow down at the end of the driveway. I stare at it. The window winds down and a woman leans out with a phone to take a photo, then the car drives off.

Some ancient jazz singer used to live in the village. She must think it was here.

Mum walks round me, to open the car boot. "What was that about?"

"The paparazzi have caught up with me," I joke as I lift out my little suitcase. "Weird though, right?"

"What's weird?" asks Steve, only just emerging from the car.

I let Mum explain. I can't be bothered.

Warm, yellowy light spills out of the kitchen window, through the half-closed blinds. That's where everyone will be.

A black, fluffy dog bounds round the side of the house and rushes towards us with an excited whine. I crouch low and he dive-bombs me, panting with delirious pleasure. I hear Auntie Gabs helloing before I see her. She emerges round the corner wearing a pale blue blanket thing, her blonde-grey hair pushed back with a red headscarf. She hugs me first.

Jakob's next to her, shivering in a thin long-sleeved floral shirt, a beanie hat low on his head. "Le-aaaah!" he says and he clasps me towards him in a funny little side-sway. He's taller, and his hair is longer, kicking out from under the hat. I smile past him at his parents, Elaine and Marc, as I rub his spindly arms to warm him. They say how good it is to see me, then look at me as if I'm not quite the person they remembered in their head. It's been a whole year, after all. Elaine is wearing her usual uniform of fleece and unflattering jeans. I'm half-surprised Marc isn't in his running gear.

Someone ruffles the top of my head and I twirl round to see Ivy. She's small and energetic, like me. Ivy plays county hockey; I dance three times a week. The golds and browns of her eyeshadow give her a new, sophisticated edge, but when she smiles I sink back into the Roeshot House comraderie.

"Make-up's on point," I say, and she laughs and embraces me.

I look for Poppy, but before I can ask where she is, Mum introduces Ivy to Steve. They shake hands (*shaking hands?*) and I want to say, *That jumper. I know.*

"You're not the only newbie, Steve," says Auntie Gabs, her voice loud with enthusiasm. "We've got my friend's sixteen-year-old daughter here too. Tatum."

I look at Ivy. The eye-rolling over Steve's jumper can wait. Why didn't I know about Tatum? Ivy gives a little shrug, as if it's not important. But it is. How can we be the Three Amigos with some new girl?

"Last-minute addition," says Auntie Gabs cheerfully. "Come and meet her. She's in the kitchen with Poppy."

"Time for cake!" says Marc, and there's laughter. There's a rule, or perhaps it's a tradition, that we can't start Marc's famous mandarin-and-chocolate cake until the last family has arrived. As I'm jostled into the house, with Elaine going on about the boiler not working, I feel the familiar excitement of having five days ahead of me with my Amigos.

TWO

The kitchen at Roeshot House was renovated a couple of years ago. The units are painted pale grey and there's a huge gleaming double oven that Auntie Gabs and Elaine went crazy over the first time they saw it. The big, wooden, slightly wobbly table wasn't replaced and there's still a mark where Jakob tried to carve a J in it with a ballpoint pen until Elaine saw him and went ballistic.

Poppy is sitting at it with an intricate colouring book and a rainbow of pens, and my mind stumbles as I take in her changed appearance from last year. She's lost so much weight her head looks too big for her body. I know via Ivy that she's had an on-off viral thing for nearly a year now, but I thought it was more like a cold she couldn't completely shake off than a thing that was causing her to waste away. She's eight, but she looks much younger.

She smiles, her front teeth almost too big for her mouth.

"Hi, Pops!" I say. "How are you doing?"

"OK," she says.

"She's got muscle ache today so doesn't want hugging," says Ivy. "It's a high-five day."

I go closer and let Poppy tap her hand against mine. Her wrist looks snappable.

"And this is Tatum," says Ivy.

The adults move out of the way and I see Tatum standing by the kettle, removing the cellophane wrapping from a box of teabags. Her hair is light brown with pink ends. But it's not just her hair which makes her striking. She has great skin, red lipstick, immaculate eyebrows and a far curvier figure than me or Ivy. I really like her oversized silvery jumper, but I know I'm too short for it to look good on me.

"Thanks for letting me scrape in," she says cheerfully. There's no part of her which looks awkward about being with a bunch of people she doesn't know.

I nod. "Hi." I hope she doesn't hear the flatness in my voice. If she's a year older than us, surely she should have lots of work to do? Unfortunately she doesn't look quiet and studious, the type to be happy writing essays in a quiet corner of the house while the Amigos are in the attic. I bet she'll want to join in.

Ivy says, "Tatum lives near us, but we're at different

schools. We used to go to a playgroup together though, didn't we?"

Tatum nods and says, "Yep, but I don't remember you at all." It has a dismissive edge.

Across the room, I hear Auntie Gabs explain that Tatum's nan had a fall so her mum had to go and help, her dad's away working and her brother is travelling. She calls out, "OK, folks, hands up for tea? Coffee?"

"I'll make Poppy's milkshake," says Ivy.

"Milkshake?" says Jakob. He picks up a glittery straw on the counter, next to a tall glass and a yellow tin with stick people doing exercises round it. "I'll have a banana milkshake too."

"You can't, it's a protein drink for building up Poppy's muscles," murmurs Ivy. She picks up the straw and jabs him playfully in the stomach. "How are your core muscles?"

"Ow," says Jakob. "I'm going to cut the cake."

Tatum plunks teabags in mugs. "Got to make myself useful," she says, and I look around for something to do too because I suddenly feel like a spare part.

Ivy shoves a packet of paper napkins in my hand. "Here. Put these out."

The napkins have reindeer on them, the arty, wispy sort. Auntie Gabs's sort of thing. In our house we just have kitchen roll. I sit at the table next to Poppy and fold them into different shapes. We make a fan and a wonky heart, and an attempt at a flower. When we've done that, she lets me do some colouring, directing me which colours to use.

"You're honoured," Ivy says as she places the milkshake in front of Poppy. "She won't let me do that."

Tatum brings the mugs over to the table and everyone else sits down in dribs and drabs. Steve positions himself next to Mum and I have to look away. That was Dad's usual seat.

Auntie Gabs says, "Clive from Pinhurst Properties is coming to fix the boiler as soon as he can. He sends his apologies."

"We should ask for a refund, or at least a discount," says Mum.

"Jakob, go and find a jumper," says Elaine. "You're making me cold just looking at you." She shivers into her brown fleece. There's photographic evidence that Elaine was once slim and fashionable, but I still find it hard to believe.

"Yeah, in a minute," says Jakob, forking a large chunk of cake into his mouth.

Marc rubs his knee. "Where's the paracetamol, Elaine?"

"No idea," she replies. "I hope you didn't rely on me to pack it."

"Marc runs marathons," Mum says to Steve.

"Can't run at the moment," says Marc with a grimace. "Hurt my knee in an accident a couple of months ago."

"He fell off the treadmill at the gym," says Elaine. She shakes her head. "Honestly."

Our low-key sniggers turn into proper laughs, and Marc pretends to be hurt. "All right, all right," he says.

"I run a bit," says Steve. "5k, mostly."

Silence. He's killed the conversation. He blushes slightly and pushes his glasses up his nose.

"I went to my first spinning class the other day," says Mum. "Anyone tried that?"

I'm grateful to Baz for snuffling up to me. I pat my thighs and he jumps his front legs up and I scoop his back ones up so that he's sitting in my lap, very pleased with himself.

"Don't let him get too close to the cake," warns Auntie Gabs.

I pull my chair back and stroke him under his chin, which blisses him out.

"He's so cute," says Tatum, leaning across to touch one of his ears. It twitches and he looks at her adoringly as if he understands what she's said.

"I'm going to make Baz a bow tie," says Poppy. She makes a fan shape out of a napkin and twists it in the middle.

I hold it against Baz's neck. "It really suits him," I say. Baz is pissed off and tries to eat the napkin, and the others laugh at my surprised face.

I tug the napkin away from him but he holds on tight. "He sometimes chokes on paper," says Poppy anxiously.

I tug some more but Baz thinks it's a game.

"Here, Baz," says Tatum. She holds out her palm with a small piece cake on it.

Baz drops the napkin immediately to wolf it down, and Ivy catches it.

Elaine says, "That dog is so greedy."

Gabs says, "Yes, he'll eat anything. No more feeding him. He's supposed to be on a diet."

"I gather you and Steve are spending a couple of nights away," says Elaine to Mum. She smiles but her tone is disapproving. That's standard for her. "What a shame. Coming all this way and then going off again."

"It's the only time we could do it," says Mum. "Leah's staying. I wouldn't be able to drag her away."

I widen my eyes at the horror of being dragged away to visit Steve's sister.

"I thought this week was about being together," says Elaine.

"Two nights, that's all," says Mum. "You won't be any bother, will you, Leah?"

Before I have a chance to say anything sarcastic, Auntie Gabs says, "None of them will be. They're all lovely. And Ivy's been a real support to me this year what with one thing and another." She glances at Poppy, who lowers her head further over her colouring.

"Well done, Ivy," says Elaine, and then spoils it by saying, "Jakob could do with being a bit more responsible."

"Cheers, Mum," says Jakob.

"Before I forget," says Auntie Gabs, "I've put Tatum in with you, Leah, if that's OK with you?"

"Oh," I say. I know she's not really asking if it's OK

with me. She's telling me. I'm not used to sharing a room and I'd have liked more of a heads-up. "Er. . ." Everyone's looking at me. There are two beds in my room. I guess it makes sense, but I hate the way Auntie Gabs is beaming at me as if having a random stranger in my room is nothing.

"It'll be fun," she says.

"It's fine," I say briskly.

"I'm having two beds this holiday," says Poppy. "One downstairs and one upstairs."

Everyone looks at Auntie Gabs.

"Tell them, Mum."

Auntie Gabs nods. "The thing is, Poppy sometimes has difficulty with stairs, so I said I'd make up an airbed for her in the little lounge next to the conservatory, and she can decide each night if she wants to sleep there or in with Ivy."

"Oh, right," says Mum. "Good idea."

"I might have a think about two beds for myself next year if Marc doesn't stop snoring," says Elaine. I think it's her attempt at lightening the mood.

Last year Poppy was running around the house like your average seven-year-old. Now she has difficulty with stairs like an elderly relative.

"We'll do the airbed now, if you want," says Ivy. She means us, the Amigos plus Tatum.

"Would you?" says Auntie Gabs. "Thank you, my lovely."

We're eager to leave the adults. Poppy comes with us, her legs stiff and fragile.

"Jakob, don't forget your violin practice," calls Elaine after us.

"Tatum's not too bad," I whisper to Ivy as we pick up the bed, duvet, pillow and fleecy blanket Auntie Gabs brought in from the car and left in the hallway.

"Yes," Ivy says. "A probationary Amigo, maybe."

I wouldn't go that far.

In the little lounge, Poppy sits on one of the stiff armchairs and watches while the rest of us assemble the bed how she likes it. She shows us the little two-way radio Auntie Gabs has borrowed for the week, with three receivers, so that she can call her mum or Ivy in the night if she needs them. When the bed's ready, Ivy suggests she tests it out, and while she's lying there, I flop down beside her and pretend to snore, then Baz joins us, followed by Jakob and Ivy, and Tatum stands over us and says, "That airbed is going to deflate any second now with all your weight on it."

We scramble off, Baz barking with excitement, Jakob searching for his hat, Ivy and me trying to get the bedding sorted again, Poppy announcing she's going back to the kitchen, and I say, "Let's go up to the attic."

THREE

We have our allotted positions. Jakob and I have a saggy sofa each, and Ivy likes to nestle down into the armchair. There are beanbags too, but we tend to use those for throwing at each other or games.

The attic's a long way from the kitchen and lounge – down a corridor, across a hallway, another corridor, up a set of stairs, along the landing to another staircase, narrower and steeper. It means the adults rarely bother us when we're up here.

We raced to keep ourselves warm, pointing out the treacherous section of loose carpet on the first set of stairs to Tatum, the Amigos jostling each other against the wall on the attic staircase, while Tatum kept a slight distance, and now Jakob is out of breath.

He points to the sofa nearest the bookshelves. "Tatum, you have that. I'll share with Leah." He bounces onto my sofa and snatches at the tartan blanket on the back of it.

"Hey!" I tussle it from him and shake it out, so that it covers both of us up to our waists as we sit at either end.

There's a blanket on the other sofa and on the armchair too. Tatum picks hers up slowly, hunched up from the cold.

"Even when the boiler works, it's freezing up here," I tell her. "At least you're wearing a jumper. Jakob should have listened to his mum."

Jakob curls up under his section of blanket and pulls his hat down even further. "I'm too cold to get a jumper. I'll die on the way."

"It's gloomy up here, even with the lights on," says Tatum. "Why aren't there any blinds or curtains?"

There's a window near the desk, a skylight that opens on to the roof, and a couple of Velux windows on the slopey part. The room could do with being cosied-up, it's true, but the sofas are comfy and there are blankets.

I point at a light bulb which has blown. "That's why it's gloomy."

"So what do you do up here?" asks Tatum. She pulls her phone from her jeans pocket. "No signal. Seriously?"

"We once got one near the desk," I say. "For about thirty seconds. Sometimes you can get one by the fridge in the kitchen, but the nearest guaranteed place is by the wall at the end of the drive."

Tatum stands up and wafts her phone around the desk, up

high then low, angling her screen so she can see it. We watch with interest but zero expectation. "Nothing," she says and returns to the sofa with a massive sigh. "No offence, but this place is a shithole. My bedroom smells of damp, and the toilet handle needs pushing down three times before it will flush."

We take a second or two to register this. Ivy straightens up in her armchair, and Jakob says, "Whoa," under his breath.

"No offence, but I don't think you had anywhere else to go, did you?" I say, letting my blanket drop a moment.

"My dad's working in Dubai. I could have gone there. Sunshine. A pool. Maid service."

"So why didn't you?" asks Jakob.

Tatum is doing something with her phone. "Mum said with Dad working it would be boring and I'd have more fun here." She looks up, hoping we get her irony.

"Give Roeshot House a chance," says Ivy.

"You need to go through the initiation ceremony," says Jakob.

Tatum places her phone down beside her. "You have an *initiation ceremony*?"

Jakob tweaks my big toe under the blanket. "Yeah, you have to drink our blood."

I nod.

Tatum's head jerks back. "What?"

Ivy and I laugh. "We once did that," Ivy says. "Sort of."

I explain that we pricked our thumbs with a needle and each added a drop of blood into half a glass of champagne we nicked from downstairs then sipped a tiny bit of it to swear allegiance to each other. "At the time it was pretty exciting. We were a lot younger."

"Ew," says Tatum. "That's vile. You might have got some disgusting disease."

"Yeah," says Jakob. "I googled it afterwards. I wouldn't do it again."

"We used to have an Amigo salute," I say. "It was the Brownie salute but with two fingers, crossed for luck. There was a sequence to it."

The three of us sit up straight and salute as one, and Ivy says, "Hmm, that was after Marc made us sit through some old war film, and Leah was into dystopian novels."

Tatum sniffs the cushion on her sofa, then places it behind her head. "What d'you do these days?"

"We always come up with something," says Ivy, which sounds vague but is the best way of explaining how it is.

"Jakob likes reading out sex scenes in books that other people have left up here," I say.

"True," says Jakob. "Very true."

"Remember when we fenced with bananas?" I say, giggling. "I was doing really well but then my banana skin split and a bit of banana landed on the floor." I point to the patch of floor near the door, and I snort as I remember, "And ... and..." I can't speak now for hysterical laughter. "She ... she..." I point at Ivy.

"I slipped on it," says Ivy and re-enacts the moment and my stomach aches from laughing.

"Right," says Tatum. She re-tucks her blanket round her feet.

I stop laughing. She's only a year older than us but she clearly thinks we're really childish.

"We do normal things too," says Jakob, "like talk, listen to music, watch films."

"And make predictions," says Ivy.

"Oooh," says Tatum, perking up finally.

"We keep them in a secret place," I say. "We tick off any that come true."

"Can I see?" asks Tatum.

"No, they're boring," says Jakob.

"Yeah," says Ivy. "They need chucking away." She can't help looking at the rug. The predictions lie underneath, in the floor cavity, accessed via a floorboard that's never fitted properly.

I bite my lip. Last year's predictions were far from boring. They freaked us out.

Tatum moans. "You guys are no fun."

"Tell us some interesting things about you, Tatum," I say. I move closer to Jakob, so I can have more blanket. He rearranges his long legs and lets me slide in between him and the back of the sofa. It's a lot warmer like this.

"Ah, so cute, you two," says Ivy. She brings out her phone to take a photo, and Jakob and I tilt our heads towards each other and pout obligingly for her.

"How many interesting things d'you want to know?" asks Tatum.

"As many as you can think of," says Ivy.

"OK..." says Tatum. "My favourite subject is Film Studies. I want to go to film school. I live in London. I've recently split up with my boyfriend because he was becoming too needy. We went out together for about eighteen months."

I've never met anyone who talked about film school as if it were a serious possibility. None of us Amigos have been out with anyone, and eighteen months – that's a considerable length of time.

"Another interesting fact: for my next birthday I'm going skydiving, a tandem jump with my dad," says Tatum.

"Wow," says Ivy.

"I'm going to wear two different cameras on my helmet," says Tatum, and she veers off into explaining which cameras.

Jakob sits up. "That's awesome."

"My dad would never do that," I say, but I shouldn't have. I don't want to think about him, and I've broken the unspoken pact. I make an apologetic face to Ivy.

She lifts a hand a tiny bit to mean *don't worry, it's OK*.

"Yup, my dad can be quite cool when he tries," says Tatum.

Jakob changes the subject, saying, "We like a good ghost story. Leah's the best at telling them. But here's the thing – she hates scary films. How does that work?"

"I'm complicated, that's how," I say.

Tatum says, "I *love* scary films." Right on cue, the

window by the desk rattles from the wind outside and there's a mournful screeching coming from somewhere. "What's that?" she asks, clutching her blanket.

Ivy and I laugh.

"A fox in the woods behind the house. Don't panic," says Jakob, the Amigo who understands the country best, even though he'd rather be living in London, New York or Milan. I live on the coast, where it's all about seagulls and mists off the sea, and people eating sandwiches in cars.

"I hate foxes," says Tatum. "They just stand and stare when I'm walking home on my own, and they chew our recycling bins. One went through a cat flap three doors down from us and we could hear our neighbour screaming from our house."

"I'd have screamed too," I say.

The sound, like someone being attacked, comes again, and I'm glad I'm inside, safe and relatively warm, wedged up against Jakob. Ivy aims a table-tennis ball for the bowl on the shelves, on the other side of the room. It lands with a hollow plastic ping followed by lots of little bouncy pings. "Yesss!" she says. There was a table-tennis table up here for a few years until the legs kept collapsing. She misses it.

"Ivy," I say cautiously. "I didn't realize Poppy was so ill. That's really tough."

Ivy seems to sink into the armchair. "Her health is up and down. I guess I haven't properly noticed her getting worse because I see her every day," she says. "It's kind of tiring looking after her though. Especially when Mum has

24

one of her days. You know, when things get too much for her."

"That sucks," says Tatum in too cheerful a voice.

"We can help you this week," I say.

"Thanks," Ivy says. "She's quite a sweet kid, really."

"Remember her panda phase?" says Jakob. "When she'd be in a strop if she couldn't wear black-and-white clothes?"

Ivy rolls her eyes. "She's out of that, thank goodness, but she's still into pandas. I've promised that when she's well enough I'll take her to see a real one in Edinburgh zoo. She loves the live panda cam."

"There's a live panda cam?" asks Tatum. She picks up her phone before remembering there's no signal and chucks it back down beside her.

Jakob shifts further down the sofa, taking too much blanket with him, and asks us what our most tragic Christmas presents were. Nothing has ever topped the Thomas the Tank Engine pyjamas (age 4–5) he was given by his godfather a couple of years ago. He brought them to Roeshot House and modelled the stretched-to-the-max top for us, but we drew the line at him leaping around in the bottoms.

We hear the sound of a gong far away. It must be an adult hitting it because there are three perfectly timed rings. If it was Poppy there would have been a frenzied bashing. Maybe she doesn't have the strength to do it any more.

"Time for dinner," Jakob says to Tatum. He throws back the blanket and rushes to gain a head start.

FOUR

I'm not surprised to see Clive in the kitchen. He owns and runs the holiday rental company Pinhurst Properties, which consists of a few holiday homes in the area. He's often here fixing things, and Elaine had said he was coming to sort out the boiler, but I'm surprised to see the boy with him. He's around our age: a real-life Pinhurst teenager. I catch the look of boredom on his face as we charge in, but he switches to a smile.

"Hi there," says Clive to us, lifting his toolbox. "Boiler's up and running again. We'll leave you good people to eat your meal in peace. It does smell nice, I must say."

"It's Elaine's signature dish," says Auntie Gabs.

I picture thick gravy spelling out Elaine's signature. I've

seen her writing on birthday and Christmas cards. It's very precise.

"Lovely to see you, Clive," says Mum. "And you, Evan."

"Yes, he's sixteen now. Time for him to earn his keep," says Clive. He laughs heartily, while Evan cringes, but in a way that suggests he gets on all right with his dad. He's not as tall as Jakob but he's sturdier. He looks down to the floor and notices that I'm wearing the same trainers as him. I smile as he raises an eyebrow in recognition.

Clive shifts his toolbox to his other hand, and Marc says, "Is business booming?"

"Not too bad," says Clive. "All things considered."

"Market not as buoyant as it was? Grown the business too fast?" Marc says.

Elaine takes hold of Marc's arm. "Food's on the table. Don't get into a long conversation."

"It's just this house," says Evan defensively. "The rest are doing well."

"Oh?" says Tatum, leaning in towards him. "Why's that? Maybe you should install Wi-Fi."

"Well, people saw the news and—" Evan suddenly freezes, as if realizing he's just made a terrible error. His face reddens as his eyes flick to his dad.

"What news?" asks Tatum.

"*Evan!*" snaps his dad.

"Sounds intriguing," says Tatum.

"Someone stopped their car to take a photo of the

house when we arrived," I say. "Did something happen here?"

Evan screws his face up. "It's nothing."

"Come on!" says Tatum. "Tell us!"

The hubbub in the kitchen fades as everyone tunes in to potentially interesting information.

"Uh-oh," says Marc, leaning back against the table to rest his knee. "Don't tell me this place was used for sex parties."

"Marc!" hisses Elaine.

Clive clears his throat. "Nothing like that. Local stuff, really."

"You can't leave us hanging," says Tatum.

"Some bones were found in the garden," says Evan slowly. He pulls his hand over his nose, embarrassed now. The rest of us move closer to hear more easily.

Mum says, "Oh, how awful."

Clive takes a deep breath. "The person – the lady – who lived here before we took the place on," he begins. He places his toolbox on the floor again. "She, er . . . she told the matron of her nursing home to look for a body in the garden."

"Did she murder someone?" asks Tatum.

"Erm, well, we're not sure yet," says Clive.

"Who was it? The body, I mean," asks Poppy from her place at the table, her voice spinning through the stillness.

Clive grimaces. "Her sister."

"How old was she?" asks Elaine.

"Ah," says Clive. He looks uncomfortable, and I realize Elaine's asked a key question. "It was way back in the fifties, but I believe she was sixteen. It may have been natural causes." We hear the doubt in his voice, as he says natural causes.

"Sixteen," echoes Ivy. "There was a *sixteen-year-old* buried in this garden and no one knew?"

"We noticed the garden had been dug up by the garage as we drove in," says Elaine. "Didn't we, Marc? We thought you were embarking on some landscaping, Clive. But, oh – *that's where the body was buried*." Her voice has become a whisper.

Clive nods. "Yes, I'm so sorry. I assumed you'd have seen it in the news. But don't let that spoil your visit; it all happened a long time ago."

"I thought you said it happened a few weeks ago," says Marc.

"I meant the death," says Clive. "Once the media interest dies down, we'll be back to business as normal."

"Right," says Marc. "Still, a bit of a shock though, mate."

"Yes," says Clive. "Of course. I understand."

"I think we should get some sort of refund. The price has shot up a lot in recent years," says Mum. A blush starts on her neck and works its way up to her cheeks. "But I know now's not the time to discuss it."

"I'm, uh, sure we can work something out. Let's chat another time. Your food will be getting cold," says Clive.

"I'll bring some wood over for the log-burning stove tomorrow. Give me a shout if there's anything else." He picks up the toolbox and the two of them leave.

Auntie Gabs puts her finger to her lips to stop us exploding into conversation until we hear Clive and Evan get into a vehicle. As soon as we hear car doors thudding shut, it begins:

A body in the garden?

She must have been murdered. Why else would you bury a body?

Why didn't anyone notice she was missing?

God, how unpleasant. No wonder business isn't booming.

I wonder if anyone was staying here at the time — can you imagine?

Who's got a phone signal?

We don't want to upset Poppy.

But it was sixty years ago.

Ah, look. It made the BBC news. How did we miss it?

Imagine keeping a secret like that all your adult life.

Yes, the best signal is always by the fridge.

I've never got a signal there.

It's taking ages to load.

Did you ask Clive if he's got plans to have Wi-Fi here?

I think it's nice that the children have a break from social media.

Yeah, right, you want Wi-Fi just as much as we do.

Jakob, d'you have to wear that hat for this meal?

We watch a short clip, crowding round Elaine's phone,

groaning when it buffers every few seconds. There's a sweeping shot of Roeshot House with a police car parked on the drive and the area around the garage taped off. The reporter, a man in a suit, says there was a deathbed confession from an elderly woman at a nursing home in the village.

She was called Alice Billings. It seems such an ordinary name for someone with a secret that big. She allegedly told staff at the nursing home where they would find the body of her sister, who died as a teenager.

A black-and-white, face-and-shoulders photo of Alice around the time of her sister's death flashes up. She has a stiff, fifties, house-wifely hairstyle and wears a dress with a collar. She could be any age between eighteen and forty. The reporter says Alice was twenty-four, married and living in Roeshot House at the time. There's another photo, not such a clear one, of her sister, Rose. She's standing – oh my God, *she's standing outside the front door of Roeshot House*, in a thick coat, holding a suitcase, and smiling happily She looks young. Is she supposed to be sixteen in this photo, or was it taken when she was younger? I'd like to study those photos, but Elaine says the food is getting cold and it's time for dinner.

We eat and talk about nothing but the logistics of how you could keep the death of your sixteen-year-old sister secret. Marc says it would be pretty much impossible these days with thermal-imaging cameras, forensic techniques, and CCTV in stations, airports and pretty much round every corner.

Auntie Gabs says that's not true. There was a case not long ago where a woman had gone into a police station to say she'd killed her father several years before, and buried him in the garden. It depended on whether anyone noticed or cared whether the person had gone missing.

Tatum says she doesn't understand why the police didn't check through the records to see if Rose had ever booked a plane ticket for Switzerland, and Mum says in those days you would probably have taken the ferry and then a train, and Tatum says same difference, they should have checked the ferry records.

Elaine says, "Why would anyone have checked if they believed Alice Billings's story?"

Steve asks if anyone's watched the TV programme *Hunted*, but no one has.

Ivy says there must have been a whole lot more unsolved crimes before people had digital footprints.

Eventually Auntie Gabs brings the wine bottle down on the table and says she's had enough. She doesn't want to dwell on this Rose or anything to do with crime any more, and we're upsetting Poppy.

We look at Poppy who says, "I don't mind," but her wobbly voice doesn't match her words.

Ivy, next to her, places her arm round Poppy's shoulder. "Sorry. We'll stop," she says.

"I'm looking forward to doing a spot of birdwatching tomorrow," says Steve.

Nobody knows how to answer that apart from Mum, who says, "Sounds great!" despite having a phobia of birds ever since one accidentally flew into our kitchen and became trapped.

After we've eaten, everyone pitches in clearing the table, stacking the dishwasher and washing up the pans. Elaine takes a tea towel and stands near Mum, who's wiping down the counters, and says in a fake-whisper, "Kate, if there's ever an issue with affording your share of this place you must just say. Marc and I will help out."

Mum stops wiping and straightens up. "You thought that because I said to Clive. . . No, I was making a general point." She tacks on "thank you, though" and returns to the marble counter, attacking a splodge of spilled slow-cooked beef.

I turn to pour the water from the glass jug down the sink, imagining it sloshing over Elaine instead, and it's followed by a prickling of guilt. Does Mum keep coming here even though we can't really afford it because she knows I like it so much?

Auntie Gabs insists on "family time" in the lounge before anyone disperses, which means games. The room still has Christmas decorations up: tinsel above the paintings of dogs and muscly horses, paper chains scalloped along one wall, and holly on the mantelpiece. Steve builds up the fire, going outside in the cold to fill the log basket, like the suck-up he is, while the rest of us fight over who gets to cuddle Baz, and what game we're going to play. For some reason I didn't quite catch, Jakob is demonstrating Irish dancing to Tatum, and the rest of us whoop and clap until he drops in a melodramatic heap on the carpet, saying he shouldn't have danced after eating so much.

Ivy comes to sit next to me and says, "Tatum was looking at Evan, did you see? I think she likes him."

"Really? You think so?" I sigh. That's not what I needed to hear. I was planning to tell Ivy we should try and see him again. I thought she'd seen that I maybe liked him too.

Eventually everyone agrees on the drawing game, our own version of Pictionary, mainly because it's Poppy's favourite. We make two teams of five by drawing names from Jakob's hat, while he uses the reflection from the glass in a painting to rearrange his hair.

We move to the other end of the lounge and sit at the dining table in two teams. I'm with Jakob's parents, Ivy and Steve. Elaine has amassed a tin full of words and phrases that initially started as her trying to expand Jakob's vocabulary. She adds new ones each year, and claims she can't remember the phrases because there are so many.

Poppy goes first on the other team, taking a folded-up piece of paper from the tin, then refolding it so no one can see it and placing it in a bowl to prevent it from being picked again. The rest of her team crowd round her as she waits for Elaine to press the timer on her phone and shout

Go. Poppy draws decisively with a pencil on the blank piece of paper in front of her: a person holding a stick.

"Conductor?" suggests Auntie Gabs.

Poppy shakes her head.

"Wizard," whispers Steve, and I glare at him because he's on our team, not theirs.

Tatum repeats it more loudly, and Poppy shakes her head. She draws little rectangles with hearts, clubs, spades and diamonds coming out of the person's other hand.

"Poker player with a cattle prod," murmurs Jakob.

"Magician!" calls Mum, and Poppy yays. Elaine checks the timer, and says, "One point."

For our team, Ivy draws a trophy followed by a jacket, drawing an arrow to the inside of the jacket. It takes me a few seconds but I guess correctly that it's the phrase "silver lining". It's a new one this year, but I guess we think in similar ways.

Tatum says she'll draw next. "Hmm," she says, as she reads her piece of paper from the tin. "This is really hard."

"It's easier for us because we've done some of these words before," says Mum.

"But we try to do them in different ways," says Auntie Gabs. "It makes it more fun when we're creative."

Mum nods. Gabs is the creative sister. She used to be a graphic designer. Mum works in admin with spreadsheets and numbers that have to match up.

Tatum draws a geometric shape. It looks like a coffin. Next to me, Ivy draws in her breath. I think of the words in the tin. We've never had "murder" or "death" or anything like that.

"Um, funeral," says Jakob. The room is so still, I can hear the scratch of the pencil on the paper.

Now she's drawn a figure of a person inside the coffin-shape. I look at Ivy and she winces. This is so inappropriate, considering what her family has gone through.

"Corpse?" asks Mum quietly.

"No," says Tatum. "Keep going."

She adds a skirt to the figure.

They try burial, dead, graveyard, Rest in Peace, coffin, grief, secret and mourning, and then they give up. "What was it?" asks Auntie Gabs as soon as the timer goes.

"Surprise," says Tatum.

"What do you mean, *surprise*?" asks Jakob.

"That was the word," says Tatum.

"How is that related to what you drew?" asks Mum. She doesn't want to mention the word coffin again.

Tatum says, "Finding out about the body being in the garden was a surprise, wasn't it?"

Nobody knows what to say apart from Poppy, who says, "I'd have drawn a person jumping out of a big birthday cake."

"That would have been far better," says Marc. "Much more in the spirit of the game."

"It was fun seeing you guess, though," says Tatum. "I added the coffin to help. I don't suppose there was a

36

coffin, though. They probably wrapped the body in a sheet or something."

I inspect my fingernails, willing her to shut up.

"Tatum, drop the subject, please," says Auntie Gabs sharply.

"Our turn now," says Elaine. "I'll draw." She leans across the other team to take the pencil from Tatum.

FIVE

My bed is freezing. Our side of the house never properly heats up even when the boiler's working. Tatum has changed into a T-shirt and leggings and is arranging her fluffy turquoise coat over her duvet. The duvet covers are new this year, white and stiff.

"You'll need socks," I say. "Just until your feet warm up the bed and then you can chuck them out."

There's a knock at the door. Ivy pops her head round. "Can I come in? It's lonely in my room without Poppy."

"Course," I say. "Tell Jakob to join us."

"I want to discuss the dead girl," says Tatum, pulling her duvet up to her chin. "I don't know why the adults are so squeamish about it."

"They don't want Poppy getting upset, and ... it's not a very nice subject," I say. I wish she'd realize how thoughtless she's being around Ivy.

"I'm sorry, but it's hands down the most interesting thing about this house," says Tatum. "Come on, Leah. You must be fascinated."

"I'd like to know *why*," I admit.

Ivy comes back with Jakob and we Amigos sit in my bed, under the duvet, squished up against my two pillows and the wall. Jakob points to the picture on the wall of Mowgli and Baloo from the film *The Jungle Book* and the three of us burst into a rendition of "The Bare Necessities", and Ivy adds in some harmony. When Tatum starts to film us, we add exaggerated expressions and arm movements.

"Love it," says Tatum when we warble the last note.

"We should so go busking with that," says Jakob.

Tatum plays us back some footage, and Ivy says, "I'm not sure we're ready for busking yet."

We wriggle around and get comfortable. "So," says Tatum. "Let's talk about the dead girl. Rose."

The vibe changes immediately, but this conversation is inevitable now that we're away from the adults and Poppy.

"Why do we think Rose died? Do we think it was natural causes, an accident, suicide or murder?"

"I vote murder," says Jakob. "Her death was covered up. Something bad must have gone down."

I look at Ivy. "I vote murder too," she says. She doesn't seem to mind talking about this.

"I don't know," I say.

Tatum says, "It's got to be murder, hasn't it? The old lady must have done it." She sits up, takes the fluffy coat from on top of her duvet and puts it on. "I'm so cold I might have to sleep in this."

"Why would she kill her sister?" asks Ivy.

"An argument gone wrong?" I suggest. "Jealousy? Something financial? Her husband might have been involved."

"It could be anything," says Tatum. "I know!" She kicks her duvet away with her feet and leaps out of bed. "I've got a brilliant idea! This is the perfect topic for a documentary. It's exactly the kind of thing I've been looking for, for my showreel. The camera on my new phone is amazing. Who's in?"

The three of us look at each other. "We won't be able to find out much," says Ivy doubtfully.

Tatum shakes her head. She sits on the edge of her bed and leans towards us. "'Course not, but it will be fun documenting bits and pieces. It'll be the journey of our time here – and when I'm home I'll keep an eye on what the police discover, and I can add stuff."

"Hmm," says Jakob. "Who decides what gets filmed? Who's going to be presenting the documentary? Just you?"

"OK," says Tatum, spreading out her hands. "How about we make this an organic process?"

I wince at the pretentiousness of it.

"Everyone can suggest ideas and have a turn speaking

to camera," continues Tatum. "I shoot some stuff, edit it, and if there's anything you're really unhappy about, you can say and we can have a discussion about it."

We look at each other.

"It'll be a really cool project," says Tatum, "and let's face it, there's not a whole heap else to do here, is there?"

"I'm in," says Jakob.

"So am I," says Ivy.

"And me," I say. We've not done anything like that before. Tatum needs to self-filter more, but it *is* a cool project.

"It's irritating we can't get Wi-Fi," says Tatum. "That's the first thing I'm going to do tomorrow – find Wi-Fi in the village and research Alice." She opens up her phone, starts typing, then stops. "Nope. Number one on the list is to film the burial site. Hey" – she lowers her phone – "we could go out now? In the dark?"

I can't think of anything worse. "Eugh."

"No way," says Jakob. "It'll be cold and horrible out there, but don't let me stop *you*."

"Ditto," says Ivy.

"You three are such wimps," says Tatum. I don't like the annoyed look she's giving us.

"The light's too bad to see anything properly," I say.

"I'm not after perfect," says Tatum. "I'm after *atmosphere*."

Jakob breathes out noisily. "In that case, lean out of the window."

We look towards the window between the two beds, at the thick curtains I had drawn as quickly as I could when I'd come into the bedroom earlier.

"Of course!" says Tatum. "This room looks out at the front garden."

We climb out of bed to see. Tatum opens the window and we gasp as the freezing, shocking air gusts in. It takes our breath for a second or two. We shiver as we peer into the darkness, even Tatum in that big coat of hers. Our eyes adjust, making out the shadows of the three cars and the garage, and the trees. I strain my eyes, but I can't tell where the grass of the front lawn changes to earth, where the body was dug up.

Although I can't see it, I can definitely feel it. There's a sombre quality to the night.

"I can see it," says Tatum. Maybe she can.

"Can you hurry up and film, if you're going to?" I say.

Tatum frowns. "I'm not sure it's quite the right. . ."

"Close the window, then," says Ivy. "It's arctic and too. . ."

She trails off, and I add, "Creepy."

Tatum pulls the window shut with a bang that makes the frame rattle. It's not a reassuring noise.

We charge back to the beds, the other two Amgios huddling close either side of me. Tatum picks her duvet off the floor and drapes it round herself. With her bright pink hair tips and turquoise coat peeking out under the white duvet, she's like an exotic bird in a snowdrift.

"Has this house ever felt weird?" asks Tatum. "Like something bad happened here?"

"No." I don't even pause before replying. "It's always felt ordinary. Better than ordinary. Special." The ceilings in this room are high, and there's a pattern round the top, a sort of engraving. I love the sink in the corner with the old mirror above it, specked and worn and elegant.

"I'm certain it's haunted," says Tatum. "By Rose or Alice. Maybe both. There's unfinished business."

"You reckon?" says Jakob. "I don't think so."

"The predictions!" says Ivy. "You think they're connected?"

I elbow them both slightly. To Tatum, I say, "We correctly predicted the year my period would start. And that Ivy would be picked for the county hockey team before she was in Year Ten."

"Remember when you predicted you'd be given a micro pig for your birthday, Leah?" gabbles Jakob. "You've been waiting a long time for that, haven't you?"

"There have been so many predictions over the years," I say. "Most of them way off beam."

"Yes, but some of them have been funny," says Jakob.

"And the others were stupid," says Ivy.

There's silence as I rearrange the duvet over our legs.

"What aren't you telling me?" says Tatum. She gets out from under her duvet and comes to perch on my bed. She doesn't seem to care there's not really enough room, or about keeping warm or finding a comfortable position.

She's kneeling, leaning towards the three of us. "Just tell me."

I look at the others and Jakob says, "Last year, on New Year's Eve, we sat on the rug upstairs within a circle of tea-lights in the attic, holding hands, our eyes closed. We tried to channel the spirits of the people who'd lived here long before Clive bought it."

We'd never heard of Alice then. Everything seems scarier now that we know.

Ivy says, "We thought it was because we'd been taking it in turns to read a book out loud that we'd found under the sofa in the lounge, like someone wanted to get rid of it but was too scared to destroy it. It was about a group of friends being lost in a wood. We thought the predictions were because of that horrible book."

"We chucked it on the fire after we finished it," says Jakob. "The cover took ages to burn – you should have seen the green flames. I thought we'd die from toxic fumes."

Tatum nods. "What were the predictions?"

We remember them, obviously, but I say vaguely, "They were pretty random."

"I've just had a thought," says Ivy as she clings to my arm. "Which bedroom d'you think Rose slept in?" She mimes a silent scream.

"The bedrooms are bigger at the other end of the house so it's bound to have been one of the ones the adults are in," says Jakob. I like how confident he sounds.

But he's quick to join in when Tatum tells us we should stand in each of the three bedrooms on our side of the house, close our eyes for about a minute and see if we can feel Rose's presence. She says that spirits stay where they have unfinished business – such as where they were killed, or where something particularly significant happened. We go together, shivering, standing close enough to hold hands, but not quite daring to because that might make it into something more.

In each room, we all feel it: a faint sense of dread.

It could have been any of them.

SIX

I expect not to sleep well, but I don't expect Tatum to snore from practically the moment I turn the light out. I lie awake and wonder if emotion soaks into the fabric of a building. I think about how emotion is energy and energy has to go somewhere, or is that false science? All I know is that I've never felt uneasy in this bedroom before. I'm almost grateful I have a roommate, even if it's Tatum.

Outside an animal is making a howling noise. Is it a fox?

I roll over and force myself to visualize different dance routines as a distraction, but it doesn't work. The noise is disturbing. A slow, cold terror pincers up my spine as I realize it's coming from *inside* the house.

"Tatum?" I whisper. "Can you hear that?"

No response.

I move towards the door. Slowly, I open it. A pale face stares at me from the other side of the landing. Every function in my body freezes. I'm unable to scream.

"*Leah?*" It's Jakob.

I breathe out heavily and wait for my heart to beat a more normal rhythm. "What are you doing?" I say. "You scared me so badly."

"I wondered what that noise was."

We're quiet for a moment. The noise has diminished to something that sounds more like sobbing and it's coming from downstairs.

"You think it could be Poppy?" asks Jakob. He shivers in his trackie bottoms and festival T-shirt.

I nod. "She has a walkie-talkie to call Auntie Gabs and Ivy. Maybe it's not working." We look at each other. The little lounge isn't *that* far away. "I guess we should see if she's OK," I say reluctantly.

"Yes, but wait. I need warmer clothes," Jakob says.

I grab a hoodie too, and my Christmas slippers, and we go downstairs, staying close together. The house smells of a different decade at night, of old wooden furniture, scented drawer-liners and musty rugs. The crying sound is louder the closer we get to the little lounge. The door is a few centimetres ajar and as I push it further open, I say, "Poppy? It's Leah. What's wrong?"

Easing myself round the door, I see she's in the middle

of a nightmare. Her hair is stuck to her forehead with sweat and her arms are twitching.

"Poppy, it's Leah and Jakob. It's OK. You're having a nightmare."

She stops abruptly, then whimpers, "Go away!" Her eyes flutter open. "What are you doing here?" she asks, confused and scared.

"You were making such a racket we couldn't sleep," I say.

Poppy breathes heavily in and out. "I saw a ghost," she says. "By the grave. I saw her when I went to the toilet. But then she disappeared. I tried calling Mum on my walkie-talkie but she didn't answer and I didn't want to wake Ivy. So I hid under my duvet. I'm waiting for morning. Is it morning?"

I attempt a reassuring nod. "No, it's not morning yet. You've had a bad dream."

"But she was real when I saw her. When I went to the toilet." Poppy rolls on to her side towards me. "I'm not making it up. She was old with long greyish hair and a long white dress. She had bare feet. It was Alice.'"

I turn to see Jakob quietly freaking by the door. "Shhh," I say to Poppy. "Go back to sleep. We can talk about this in the morning."

"Will you stay with me until I go to sleep?" she asks. "Please."

"Sure." I smooth her hair back from her damp forehead and plump up her duvet round her shoulders.

She moves on to her side and keeps checking to see if I'm still there.

By the door, Jakob mimes that he's hungry. I mime back that he should go to the kitchen and find some food and I'll meet him there once Poppy's asleep.

It takes literal hand-holding for Poppy to be sure I'm still there, but gradually her hand slackens in mine and I hear the slow breaths of sleep. Moving quietly, I edge out of the room, then sprint to the kitchen where Jakob is sitting up on the counter eating crisps, Baz sitting on the floor watching him intently, his head on one side.

"What did she mean, a ghost?" he says, offering me a crisp.

I shake my head and crouch down to snuggle Baz. "It's not surprising after today that she thinks she saw one," I say.

"I suppose," says Jakob. He finishes the last few crisps, jumps down from the counter and chucks the packet in the bin. "She seems in a bad way this year, doesn't she? She's changed so much."

"You think it's something to do with ... you know?" I ask. He knows I mean my uncle's heart attack. "Like a delayed response?" Poppy was the one who found him dead at his desk at home.

"Maybe," says Jakob.

"D'you think we should include her more this year," I say.

"Sure," says Jakob. "She loved doing the predictions last year."

"Not that sort of thing," I say. "She made that last prediction too creepy. We don't want her involved with the documentary stuff. I meant generally spending more time with her."

He nods. "Good plan." He strokes his jawline with both hands. "I think I've got the bone structure for presenting a documentary, don't you?"

"Definitely," I say. "But at the risk of sounding bitchy, I reckon there's only room for one star in that documentary."

"Oooh," says Jakob. "I'm going to tell her you said that."

"I dare you!" I say.

He laughs. "Imagine playing twenty-one dares with Tatum. We so have to."

I'm woken the next morning by the sound of the house waking up, clanking pipes, and a ticking noise from the radiator. Tatum is still asleep, her fluffy coat on the floor, next to discarded bed socks.

Out of habit I check my phone. At least it can still tell the time even if it can't get any signal. 9:25.

I ease out of bed, tunnel into my thickest jumper, pull on Christmas slippers and flick back one side of the curtains. It's misty and grey, but I can see part of the burial site now it's light.

It has the appearance of a newly dug flowerbed that hasn't been planted yet. All the years we've been coming here, the garden has been holding a secret. We Amigos played tag on the front lawn, practised handstands and cartwheels when the ground wasn't too cold for our hands. We literally danced on someone's grave.

Tatum shifts in bed. I become a statue. I'm not ready to interact with her yet, or hear her go on again about the dead girl. When she's been still for a few seconds, I let the curtain fall back, and go to the bathroom. The shower door is wet, which means Ivy or Jakob must be up, and I know which one it's more likely to be.

Breakfast is my favourite meal at Roeshot House. There's a wide choice of cereals, breads and jams or ingredients for a full English. Sometimes there are pastries if anyone's been to the bakery in Riddingham, the nearest town, the day before.

When I'm downstairs I hear clattering from the kitchen, and Baz pads out into the hall to greet me.

"Who's that?" calls Ivy.

"Only me," I say as I carry Baz back in like a baby. He tries to lick my face. "Ew. You're disgusting," I laugh as I put him down.

"Good morning to you too," says Ivy, who's cutting an orange in two on the big chopping board by the sink.

"Baz, not you." I see Poppy sitting at the table, the hood of her white dressing-gown up. It's a panda design, with ears on the hood, black sleeves, and white everywhere else. It makes her look younger than eight. "Oh, hi, Poppy!"

She's still half asleep.

"D'you remember having a nightmare?"

Poppy nods but says nothing.

"What happened?" asks Ivy.

"She was crying in her sleep," I say. "Jakob and I both heard her and went downstairs, and I stayed with her until she went back to sleep."

Poppy says, "I had a nightmare because of the ghost."

"A ghost?" says Ivy. We lock eyes.

"Tell Ivy about the ghost," I say.

Using pretty much the same words as she told me in the night, Poppy describes the long greyish hair, white dress and bare feet.

Ivy says, "You should have used the walkie-talkie or come and got me."

"Your mum didn't hear it and she didn't want to wake you," I say.

"Oh, Poppy!" says Ivy, breathing out heavily. "Why not?"

Poppy pulls the sleeves of her dressing-gown over her hands.

"Did you think I wouldn't believe you?" says Ivy. "If you think you saw a ghost, you saw a ghost. But, you know, it might have been in your imagination or a dream. It just *felt* real."

"I was awake. I was in the downstairs toilet. It was real," insists Poppy, to the table.

"Then I believe you," says Ivy, too quickly for it to sound convincing. "Your juice is coming right up." She brings a glass over to the table. "Want one, Leah?"

I nod. "Thanks."

"Can you fetch Poppy's cereal?" says Ivy. "It's in the larder. A Tupperware container on the second shelf up with her name on."

The walk-in larder is a magical place. It's piled high with food, chocolate, speciality biscuits, and things that we only ever have at New Year. There are different-coloured glass bottles of drink with lovely labels, and party poppers, bunting and napkins for New Year's Eve. This year it seems there's a whole shelf devoted to Poppy: seeds and protein powders, supplements, cereal bars, and tubs of dairy-free milkshake powder. I spy a Lock 'n' Lock of granola with *Poppy* written in marker pen on the top.

"Thanks," says Ivy when I emerge with it. She swaps the glass of juice in her hand for the plastic container, opening it up and tipping the granola into a bowl. She pours over soya milk and places it in front of Poppy with a spoon.

"I'm not hungry," murmurs Poppy, prodding at the cereal, and leaving the spoon in the bowl.

"Let's have some juice," I say, holding up my glass. "Cheers!" I wait for her to clink my glass, and we both take a sip.

Poppy wrinkles up her face. "I don't like it."

I can't remember how fussy I was at eight. Surely not this bad?

"Morning, crew!" says Jakob. He's in his trackies and a purple sweatshirt. "Mum's only gone and woken me up.

She wants me to do some maths revision before we go to Chandler's Hill. God, she's exhausting. Any bacon?" He looks round hopefully as if ready-fried bacon might appear. "Who's been down, apart from you lot?"

"In the fridge," says Ivy. "All the adults apart from Mum. Haven't seen Tatum."

"She's still asleep," I say.

"Anyone for a bacon sandwich?" asks Jakob. He takes the clean frying pan from the draining board.

"I'm having a croissant," I say. "What about you, Ivy?"

Ivy shrugs, and settles on a croissant too. She doesn't look as if she particularly cares what she eats. I feel sorry for her. After her dad died, Auntie Gabs kind of lost it for a bit, and now Poppy's ill. She has a lot going on.

I think about the time Mum and I were arguing and I told her I wished I'd been born into their family, not ours. It wasn't just that they never seemed to worry about money. They visited quirky places on holiday and went to exhibitions of people they knew, and had stories to tell about dog shows, festivals and funny road trips. That's definitely not the case now.

Now Ivy has to look after Poppy, and make sure Gabs doesn't get too tired and stressed.

"At least it's not raining for Chandler's Hill," says Jakob, as he pokes at his bacon.

The tradition of going up Chandler's Hill on the first full day of the holiday for fresh air and exercise isn't too bad if we Amigos keep apart from the adults and stuff enough snacks into our pockets. And if the rain holds off. The walk takes place in any weather. Jakob's family own waterproof trousers and his parents are never embarrassed to be seen in them.

"I'm not going," says Poppy. "Mum's going to stay here with me."

"I don't mind staying with you," says Ivy.

Nobody's ever stayed behind before. When Poppy was a baby she was lugged on her dad's back in a baby carrier, and when she was a toddler she was bribed with biscuits and went on people's shoulders. Then there were years where she ran ahead to hide Sylvanian Families for us to find.

"I'll stay too if you want," I say. I mean it, but it feels wrong.

Poppy doesn't say anything. I watch how she pushes the granola round her bowl.

"How's school?" I ask.

"All right," she says. "But I don't go every day. When I wake up I see if I feel OK or not, then Mum and I decide. Sometimes I do half days."

"Why aren't you eating your cereal?" asks Jakob. "You want a bacon sandwich?"

"She's supposed to eat that cereal," says Ivy.

Poppy half-fills her spoon. "The doctors haven't figured out what's wrong with me yet, but they will," she says. "It's not in my head, though." Her spoon is halfway to her mouth, and she holds it there, steady. "One doctor said it was, but he's wrong."

I nod.

"My stomach hurts," says Poppy. "I can't eat it."

"I wouldn't be able to eat it either," says Jakob. "It looks like. . ." He trails off when he sees Ivy's exasperated face. "How about one of your milkshakes? Are you allowed that?"

"She is, but she should really eat that," says Ivy.

"Oh, go on, it's the holidays, and no one's allowed to have a bad time at Roeshot House, apart from me when I'm being made to do maths revision or violin practice," says Jakob. "I'll make it for her."

"It's all right," says Ivy. "I'll make you one, Pops. Banana?"

Poppy smiles and I feel a burst of happiness. Warm kitchen, Amigos. I could hug Jakob.

Baz stands up, his ears raised. He can hear someone coming. It's the person I least want it to be:

He's wearing awful jeans, even worse than Elaine's, and a strangely shiny burgundy jumper that's too tight, in a shrunk-in-the-washing-machine way rather than a muscle-bulging way. "Morning," he says. "I'm looking for my binoculars. I know I brought them in from the car yesterday. They're in a black case. You haven't seen them, have you?" He makes circles with his forefingers and thumbs and brings them up to his glasses as a visual prompt. As if we don't know what binoculars are.

Poppy shakes her head, Ivy looks around vaguely, as if there might be a black case next to the juicer, and I ignore him.

"They must be somewhere," he says. He pushes his glasses up the bridge of his nose and wanders into the lounge.

"Of course they're *somewhere*," I mutter. "Sorry about him."

Poppy is staring at me. I hope she's not going to ask about Steve and Mum's relationship or whether I like him, or in fact anything about him at all.

"Tatum snores," I say. It's the first thing that comes into my head.

It brings a smile to Poppy's face. "Are you going to let her be an Amigo?" she asks.

I make a horror-face without thinking, and Poppy laughs.

There was a big row once about us not letting Poppy be an Amigo when she kept barging in on us in the attic. We ended up telling her that she could only be one when she was a teenager. It felt like a sufficiently long way off.

I say, "We'll have to see."

SEVEN

Auntie Gabs is next into the kitchen. She's dressed but yawning, her hair held on top of her head with an enormous clip. "Good morning, everyone," she says. She gives Steve a more welcoming smile than he deserves as he wanders back in. "Did you all sleep OK?"

Everyone says yes, except for Poppy who tells her mum about the ghost, while Ivy makes her mum a cup of tea, then stirs the milkshake vigorously, clacking the spoon against the glass.

Steve stops looking for his lost binoculars on the coat hooks and listens to Poppy's description of the ghost.

Auntie Gabs rubs her forehead, as if she has the beginning of a headache. "Oh, Poppy, I'm sorry I didn't hear the walkie-talkie. I'll check the volume on it. Promise me you'll try it again if you need me?"

Her attention turns to what Poppy's had to eat, and Ivy gives Poppy the milkshake and the glittery straw, and Auntie Gabs takes away the cereal without saying anything. Poppy picks up the straw and dunks it in the yellow liquid, pulls it out and licks the end. She's only eight, but I've heard of really young children having eating disorders.

Jakob chomps down the rest of his sandwich, goes into the larder to find one of the silver straws for New Year's Eve, cuts it with scissors to make a pair of fangs and acts out being a vampire. This involves grabbing me and pretending to suck blood from my neck. Next he waggles his arms around and goes towards Poppy's milkshake.

"Let me suck up your lifegiving juice," he cackles, staggering over to the table. He dunks his head down so the straws dip into the glass.

"Watch out. The table's wobbly," says Ivy, attempting to hold it steady. It lurches, the glass crashes over, and the yellowy liquid spills rapidly in two directions. We all shriek and stand, scraping our chairs back as it drips over the edge of the table on to the floor.

"I'm sorry! I'm sorry!" says Jakob, nearly tripping over Baz, who's come to lap it up. "I'll get a cloth."

Ivy uses kitchen towel and dishcloths to soak up the milkshake on the table. "Ew. There's so much of it," she says.

"It's no problemo for me to mop the floor," says Steve. He seems to know where the mop's kept. "Nobody got soaked, did they?"

I feel cold wetness seeping through my left slipper, but I don't need Steve to fuss over me or take it to the airing cupboard to dry off.

"Look, Baz is making paw prints round the kitchen," says Poppy with delight as he scampers back and forth through the liquid as if it's an irresistible outdoor puddle. She places a tea towel on the floor and manages to coax him on to it to dry off his paws, while Steve hurriedly mops. When calm is restored, the two of them high-five each other with unnecessary loudness.

Mum appears, then Elaine and Marc and somebody makes a large cafetière of coffee, and we Amigos do a word search with Poppy as she nibbles round the edges of a cereal bar.

Marc comments on the wine bottles lined up by the back door from last night, and Jakob looks up from the word search and says, "I'll put them in the recycling."

Ivy gives me a what's-he-up-to look, and he flashes us a half-smile as he slips his feet into his mum's squelchy shoes, and scoops up the bottles to take them to the recycling crate in the covered wood store. We hear the smash of him lobbing the bottles into the crate above the noise of the adults' conversation, and then it goes quiet for a bit. He returns with a flushed face from the cold, looking very pleased with himself.

"Come over here," he hisses, beckoning us over. "The paper recycling hasn't been emptied for ages. There are loads of local newspapers."

"Oooh," says Ivy, giving him the thumbs up.

"I need a hand taking the crate up to the attic," says Jakob.

"I'll do it," I say to Ivy. I look for shoes to put on. Steve's trainers are the only ones available to me, neatly positioned with the laces tucked inside. I'd rather wreck my Christmas slippers further. "Let's go," I say and we slip out together up the path.

The crate of *Pinhurst and Riddingham Gazettes* is heavier than it looks. We take an end each and shuffle back along to the front door, damp soaking through to both feet. The newspaper on top is about the local council turning down planning permission for a block of flats.

"I hope there's more interesting stuff underneath," I say.

"What have you got there?" asks Elaine as we come back in.

"We need newspaper for a project," I say.

"Don't make too much of a mess in the attic," says Marc. Like he ever goes up there.

Jakob and I keep moving through the kitchen to the corridor, my slippers making footprints on the old wooden flooring. At least they're not milkshake ones. Ivy follows us, helping us on the stairs.

As we go past my bedroom, Tatum emerges in her turquoise coat.

"Morning. What's that you've got?" she asks.

"Hi," says Jakob. He indicates for us to put the crate down. "I've made a brilliant discovery! Local newspapers. Potential information about Alice and Rose. We're taking them up to the attic."

"Jakob, I love you!" says Tatum. "Wow. That's so good. That's going to be perfect." She pulls her phone from out of the coat pocket and films a few seconds of the crate, leafing through the papers with her spare hand, and holding one up that says *Human Remains Found in Pinhurst*. She says, in a totally new, melodramatic voice, "Finding information was hard without easy access to Wi-Fi, but we discovered just what we needed: local newspapers." When she's stopped recording she says, "Don't start without me. I'm going to make a cup of tea and bring it up."

"*We* discovered?" says Jakob quietly after Tatum's gone. I roll my eyes.

"Hmm," says Ivy, "and that voice."

We carry the crate with difficulty up the steep attic stairs and dump it on top of the rug, and I collapse on my sofa – well, mine and Jakob's now that Tatum has temporary ownership of Jakob's. "My back hurts," I moan.

We wait fifteen minutes for Tatum, not concentrating on any conversation we start because it's hard to think of anything other than the papers there in the middle of the three of us. I go through some ballet warm-ups, holding on to the back of the sofa for a barre, and Ivy and Jakob test riddles out on each other.

I'm the one who cracks. I take the first paper, and leaf through it rapidly.

Ivy shrugs and joins in, and by the time Tatum comes upstairs the three of us have a pile of five newspapers which have relevant information in, and I've been down to my room to get some paper and a pen. I carry on writing *things we know so far* at the top of a piece of paper.

"Nooo," Tatum says, dragging out the word. "I wanted to film the sorting. Why didn't you wait? I asked you."

"Sorry," says Ivy. "You took too long."

"I was forced to listen to Poppy's story about Jakob spilling a milkshake and Baz rolling in it. Something like that anyway," says Tatum.

"We wanted to get on with it," I say without looking at her. "You can recreate the sorting if you want to."

Tatum sighs loudly. "Yes, I'll have to. I'm trying to create a narrative. Jakob, stand there and pull out papers from the crate."

Jakob does as she says.

"Work those cheekbones," I say.

Tatum directs her shoot while I doodle round the edge of my piece of paper out of shot and occasionally glance across at Ivy when Tatum's voiceover is particularly excruciating.

Finally we get down to the actual articles. What we learn is:

- In the few minutes before her death, Alice Billings told the matron at a nursing home in Pinhurst (called Silverways) that there was a body buried in the garden of her old house.
- When the police investigated, the body of a young woman was discovered.
- The body is believed to be that of Alice's younger sister, Rose Strathmortimer. It is thought she died in 1958, aged sixteen.
- A local resident, who declined to be named, said Alice told him Rose had moved to Switzerland in the summer of 1958 to be a lady's companion. Later he was told that Rose had lost touch with the family following a broken engagement.
- At the time of the death, Alice was living at Roeshot House with her husband Doug, a senior partner at Billings and Billings accountancy firm. Doug died in 1961 and Alice never remarried. They had a son, John, who is in the music business and lives in America. He is said to be shocked at the news but was unavailable for comment.
- *The Gazette* is awaiting the results of tests that will confirm the cause of death.

There's also an article about Alice winning prizes for her gardening and being involved with local charities. We pore over the photo of her being presented with a trophy for the most fragrant rose in show at the Pinhurst Flower show in 2010. She has short white hair and a cardigan with daisies on it, and she's smiling.

"It's no coincidence Alice loved growing roses, is it?" I say.

"Question is," says Tatum, "was she doing it because she wanted to remember her sister, or was it a private joke?"

"That's sick," says Jakob. "Let me look at that photo of her again. She looks so *normal*."

Tatum records herself reading out the list, but when she's on the part about Alice's son John being unavailable for comment, Elaine shouts up the stairs that we need to get dressed for the Chandler's Hill walk.

EIGHT

Once we're dressed and ready, we're desperate to go outside to film the grave in daylight. We don't want to wait for the adults to find their walking socks and appropriate footwear, or confer with Gabs about her getting a head start with tonight's meal since she's insisted on staying behind.

We say goodbye to Poppy, who's cutting out paper people, the sort who hold hands when you open them up, and tell the adults we'll take Baz and meet them outside. Ever since Baz saw Ivy with his lead, he's been circling us in a frenzy of excitement. He rushes out of the back door and we run after him, laughing at his craziness. As we come out of the side passage and see the front garden, the atmosphere changes. We're in sight of the place where Rose was buried.

We stick together. I'm nervous: what if something was left behind? I know the police will have taken everything they dug up away in evidence bags, and Clive will have checked it over afterwards. Things can be missed, though, and I think of the essence of Rose, seeped into the ground. We stand solemnly next to the large rectangle of fresh earth. We fall silent until Baz walks on it, sniffing, and we shoo him off it, embarrassed by his disrespect and worried he might begin digging, or lift his leg to pee. He sits by Poppy and does ugly dog-coughing instead.

I was expecting there to be something here to acknowledge Rose – a bunch of flowers, or a candle – but that probably wouldn't set the right holiday vibe.

"Why would you bury a body in the front garden?" asks Jakob. "You'd risk being seen by someone coming up the drive."

"The layout of the garden might have been different," I say.

"I bet the garage wasn't here in 1958," says Ivy.

"It's barely here now," says Jakob, surveying the dilapidated building with its missing roof tiles and dented metal door that doesn't hang straight. We've been in the garage a few times, but only via the side door. It's like a junk shop inside.

"Look!" I say. "That's a rose, isn't it?" Covering the side of the garage are prickly stems, leafless, skinny and brown, like a sprawling sort of skeleton. "This doesn't seem like a private joke. It seems like a not-wanting-to-forget her sister thing."

I'm aware of Tatum standing close, holding her phone towards me.

"What are you doing?" I ask. "Are you filming me? That's not fair. Warn me first."

She stops. "I thought we all liked the idea of a documentary? I need natural footage."

I look from Ivy to Jakob.

"You need to tell us," I say. "We don't want to look stupid."

"I can edit stupid stuff out," says Tatum. "But OK." She waits a moment, then says in a slow, exaggerated way, "I'm going to film a short segment now." She lifts her phone. "Filming in five, four, three, two, one. This is where Rose Strathmortimer was laid to rest in 1958 in circumstances that remain unclear. Was she buried in a rush or was it done carefully? Was it at night or in full daylight? Who was there?" She pans round and I look away. "Okaaaaay. All done."

We stand in silence, wiggling our feet around, aware now of the temperature. The clomping of boots along the side passage sounds eerie until we see Elaine, Marc, Mum and Steve emerge. At first I think Mum and Steve are holding hands, but they just happen to be standing quite close to each other. Steve has his binoculars round his neck.

"Looks like Steve found them, then," says Ivy.

"Huh?" asks Tatum.

"Steve's beloved binoculars. He's a birdwatcher," I say. "Don't go there."

Elaine shouts to us, "Stop being morbid, move away from there. There's nothing to see." She marches over anyway, with the other three, who are curious but don't want to look as if they are.

"Imagine," Marc says, "knowing your own sister was buried in your garden and not telling anyone your whole life. How could you keep that a secret?"

We spent most of yesterday evening imagining this. I think of the photo of Alice smiling at the flower show. She must have found a way of pushing it to the back of her mind, and getting on with her life.

"She must have hated her sister," says Ivy.

"But if she properly hated her, she wouldn't have said anything," said Jakob. "Or was she sticking two fingers up to the authorities?"

"Let's not dwell on it," says Elaine. She looks at her watch. "It's none of our concern. We should get moving."

"We'll probably never know the story behind it," says Mum.

Tatum looks as if she's about to tell her that we plan to find out as much as we can, but I widen my eyes and do a shake of my head, to say *Don't involve the adults*.

We head off down the driveway. As usual the adults

69

lead the way, and the Amigos drag along behind. I see Poppy watching us through the blinds at the kitchen window. I give her a wave and she waves back.

Steve attempts to hang back to walk with me, but I slow almost to a standstill, discussing with Jakob the last series we binge-watched. It takes a while for Steve to take the hint, but he gravitates back to the adults and Elaine's loud conversation about black mould in her washing machine.

We take the scenic route to Pinhurst, taking a footpath across a couple of the fields. Near the pub in the village there's always a good signal, and if we're in range we can hook up to their free Wi-Fi. We tell Tatum they haven't changed their password since we went there for a meal several years ago, and her eyes light up.

"Can we stop?" asks Tatum. "I want to check my phone."

"Two minutes tops," says Marc. "This is a walk. We're enjoying what the countryside has to offer."

Those of us under forty check our phones while the adults moan about phone addictions. I have an excited message from my friend Sofia telling me she finally got off with Dan last night at her drama club, the boy she's fancied since she joined. I tell her how pleased I am, but wonder to myself how it'll impact our friendship. Will she still have time to hang out with me? There's a text from Dad – *How's R House? I could do with a slice of Marc's lemon cake right now. Love from me and Amber x*

Mandarin and chocolate, I reply. The casual way he's forgotten the flavour of the cake upsets me.

"Let's look up Alice Billings and Rose Strathmortimer," says Tatum.

I look over her shoulder. There's no more information than we already know, except a reporter has been looking up Alice and Rose's family and discovered that the Strathmortimers were an aristocratic family who were left in "financially reduced circumstances" after Alice and Rose's father made some bad investments and died young.

There's the sound of a car slowing down and I glance up to see a four-by-four with a trailer of logs stopping by the adults. It has *Pinhurst Properties* in large letters across its side. Clive leaps out and checks with Marc that the boiler's still working, and says he and Evan are off to rescue some holidaymakers who've locked themselves out of their cottage, and then they'll deliver some logs to Roeshot House.

Evan lowers the passenger-seat window and says, "Hey, how's it going?" His smile is startling. It encompasses the four of us. "I hope I didn't freak you lot out yesterday about the..." He smiles awkwardly. "The dead body. I felt bad afterwards."

"No worries," says Tatum. "We're not traumatized."

"We'd have found out anyway, I'm sure," says Ivy.

"Phew," says Evan.

Marc yells, "OK, troops! Let's go! On to Chandler's Hill."

"Have fun!" calls Evan and waves as the car moves off. "See you later," responds Tatum.

I'm never sure how things evolve into tradition at Roeshot House. I imagine with Chandler's Hill the adults trudged to the top two years in a row and the third year someone said, "Are we going up Chandler's Hill again?" We Amigos couldn't care less about the view at the top, but the adults like to make a big deal of it. The bits that interest us are the Wi-Fi outside the pub, the stream with perilous stepping stones, the steep gravel slope on the way up the hill that you can slide down, and the triangulation pillar at the top.

The adults must have started the tradition of climbing on the triangulation pillar, and I never understood why the pillar had four sides and wasn't a triangle, or how it could ever have been used to measure the land for a map. Even when we were little, we were hoisted up so we could jump down. It felt really high up and scary. Now we still get a thrill, but it's from balancing on such a small surface area on the top. I find it easier than the other two, probably because of my dance training. We like to strike poses as we jump off and there are some classic Amigo shots in existence, of ballooned jackets in the wind, rain-drenched faces and out-and-out panic of falling before being ready.

Up ahead Steve has stopped walking and is pointing his binoculars at a bird. A blur of brown with wide wings.

"Sparrowhawk," he says as we come level with him.

"Bird of prey?" asks Ivy with more politeness than I can dredge up.

Steve nods. "Yes. Look how it gives a few wing beats then glides, going quite close to the ground. They're secretive birds, relying on surprise to catch their prey."

"Do they eat sparrows?" asks Ivy.

"Yes," says Steve. "And other small birds. Sometimes birds as large as pigeons."

I pull a face. "Gross."

We walk on, Steve tagging along with us, and as the sparrowhawk swoops, Steve whips his binoculars up to his face again. "It's got something."

I shudder and look the other way, at the sky that's darker in the distance, threatening heavy rain, while Steve goes on about wingspans and beak shapes.

The actual hill is still a way off, but we're at the stile that marks the start of the Chandler land. There's a bunch-up because of Marc's dodgy knee. He's manoeuvring his leg as if it's a new addition to his body that he hasn't got used to yet.

"Ouch," says Tatum loudly. "That hurt." She leans over, clutching her hands together.

"What have you done?" asks Elaine. "Show us."

Tatum holds up her hand. There's blood all over the fleshy part of her hand, below her little finger.

"Oh no," says Mum. She rushes over with a crumpled tissue. "It's not as bad as it looks," she says. "A superficial cut."

"I must have done it on the fence," Tatum says.

"We'll find you a plaster when we get back," Elaine says.

"I'd like to go back now," says Tatum. "I remember the way."

"Honestly," says Elaine. "You'll be fine. Marc's battling on with his knee."

"No offence," says Tatum, "but an open wound is different."

I can't help thinking she might have done this so she can go back to the spot near the pub for Wi-Fi.

"I'll come back with you," says Ivy.

"Me too," I say. "The four of us could go."

Mum shakes her head. "Tatum, you go back with Ivy, if that's what you want. Leah and Jakob, stay with us."

I could argue, but there'd be a scene, and that rarely happens at Roeshot House. When we're in Pinhurst there's a code I've become aware of over the years. I don't show Mum up in front of Auntie Gabs or Elaine, as if they're still the older kids who look down on her.

I don't say anything as the other two leave, but I glare at Mum before we carry on. I stick with Jakob, and do my best not to look at Steve, who keeps stopping to swivel round with his binoculars for murderous wildlife.

When we reach the triangulation pillar, Jakob helps me up, and lets go of my hand so I can stand upright. I teeter on the edge, holding in my stomach muscles for elongated seconds, waiting for the moment when falling is inevitable.

I love the swoop of adrenaline as my body prepares for disaster, and I visualize my theatrical pose, springing off as high as I can, imagining coils on the soles of my trainers. I don't pull off the facial expression quite how I want because I can't help breaking into a smile.

Jakob films me, adding whoops and a general standard of eccentric filming that Tatum would be horrified by.

I land elegantly, like a dancer should. Jakob stops filming, and awards me a couple of Munchies from an old stub of a packet containing just three. The caramel in the middle is solid from the cold. I help Jakob on to the triangulation pillar, which is hard because he's so much taller, and Elaine starts squealing about there not being long until his violin exam and to be careful. He does a rubbish jump, and then we run to the gravel slope and surf down, screaming about the little stones that find their way into our shoes, laughing when our bums hit the slope too soon. We're an Amigo down, but it's still fun.

NINE

When we arrive back at the house, Auntie Gabs informs us that Tatum's hand wound is nothing to worry about.

"Tell Evan he can stay for lunch if he wants," says Auntie Gabs.

"Evan?"

"Yes, he stayed after he and his father dropped off the logs. He's outside with Ivy and Tatum."

Did I get it wrong? Did Tatum cut her hand so she could be back here with Evan?

Jakob and I go back outside, to the garden. The three of them are on the trampoline. Tatum is sitting next to Evan, and Ivy's opposite them.

"How's your hand?" I say pointedly to Tatum.

"Quite sore, actually," she says, and holds it up for me to see the big plaster on it.

Evan pats the trampoline. "Come on up, you two."

I tell him he's invited to lunch as I sit between Jakob and Ivy. I notice Tatum takes the opportunity to move even closer to Evan. "What have we missed?" I ask. "Have you been talking about Alice and Rose?"

"I don't know any more than you do," says Evan. "The police haven't said anything for a while."

"*But*," says Tatum, with an added pause for emphasis, "Evan's going to do me a big favour. His mum's friend works in Silverways, the care home, and he's going to ask her if we can go and talk to her."

"Seriously?" says Jakob.

"That would be brilliant," I say. "Is she allowed to talk to us?"

"Well done, Leah!" says Tatum sarcastically. "You'll put Evan off asking her."

He shrugs at me. "I'll see what Donna says. She wasn't there when Alice died, but she'd be a good person for your documentary. She could tell you about Alice. As long as you promise to keep it quiet from my dad. He's still annoyed about me telling you."

"Did you ever meet Alice?" I ask.

"I don't remember ever speaking to her," he says, "but I knew who she was. Everyone living in the village knows each other, pretty much. She was one of those people who run things. You know, village fairs and stuff?"

We nod. I'm thinking of the photo of Alice in her daisy cardigan.

"My sister says she saw Alice's ghost last night," says Ivy. Her tone is cautious.

"What?" explodes Tatum. "Why didn't you tell me?" She demands the details, then asks Evan if Alice ever had long hair like the ghost.

"I don't know," he says. "Maybe?"

Tatum tilts her head to the end of the garden. "Those woods there – Alice would have had easy access to them. Did the police do any digging there?"

Evan shakes his head. "That's private land, owned by someone else. Anyway, the police were only looking for one body."

"Ah, right," says Tatum. "They just look kind of sinister. How do the police know there aren't more bodies? What if she was a serial killer?"

"Those woods? Sinister?" Evan turns to look at them. "Nah. And nobody thinks Alice was a serial killer."

I huddle into my coat. "D'you remember telling us there were landmines in the woods, Jakob?"

He smiles. "That's because I didn't want to go in there. Not after that time we played spies and got lost."

"Sounds like a good place to do some filming at some point," says Tatum. She pulls her phone from her pocket. "I need to interview you, Evan, about this house, and what you know. I think you'll be a natural on camera."

I hate the little laugh she does after saying this.

"Were you an eyewitness to the body being dug up? Anything like that?" Tatum continues.

Evan breathes out with a sort of laugh. "Eyewitness? Only reporters and TV people were allowed up the driveway. There were some rubberneckers in the field trying to get a look, but nah. To be honest, seeing that pop-up forensics tent made me feel..." He clutches his stomach and mimes being sick. "But I can tell you about the house."

"Great!" Tatum swipes her screen and accesses her video. "Happy to do this right now?"

"Go on, then," he says, shifting himself on the trampoline so he's a little more upright. The rest of us shuffle out of the way.

Tatum coughs then presses record. "Evan from Pinhurst Properties, the company that rents out Alice's Billings's old home, tells us about the house and garden where the body of Rose Strathmortimer was found."

Evan grins and it's a full second before he says, "Hello."

"Evan, what was the house like when your dad's company took over?"

"It was about twenty years ago, so I hadn't been born then. Dad bought the place from Alice after he promised her he would keep it as a house and garden and not try and develop it before she died."

"Aha," says Ivy. "We know the reason why."

Tatum glares at her for interrupting.

Evan nods. "She sold a lot of the furniture to my dad

79

because she didn't have room for it in the bungalow and her son didn't want it, you know, before she went to the nursing home." Evan looks at me, straight past Tatum and at me, and I smile and do a raised eyebrow, nodding thing, meaning *Go on. Add something else.* He's not as much of a natural when the camera's on him as Tatum led him to believe, but that doesn't make him any less attractive.

"So, er, the big desk in the attic, that was Alice's husband's, and some of the beds were hers, and a couple of wardrobes and a few pictures. The house is pretty much the same as when she left and, um, so's the garden. My dad's sort of doing things slowly because we have other properties and, well, cash flow. Hey, I've just remembered—" He stops, momentarily distracted, and we notice Steve standing a few metres away, watching us.

"Gabs sent me out here to say lunch is ready," Steve says. He blinks, unsure whether or not to wait for us.

"Thanks. We'll be there in a minute," says Tatum. She reviews what she's filmed, stopping it before the interruption, and jumps down from the trampoline. "That was really good, Evan, thanks. I told you the camera would love you." She is so annoying.

"What were you going to say?" I ask Evan.

"There's a book in the attic. There *was* a book in the attic, not sure if it's still there. About local gardens. *Super* boring, right? I remember Dad pointing it out to me once. He thought someone renting the house might be interested, and I said, 'You must be joking,' and Dad said, 'Just put it back on the shelf.'"

We're puzzled until he says, "The garden at Roeshot House is in there. Photos of how it was years ago. You should see if you can find the book."

"We'll look for it straight after lunch," says Tatum.

Lunch is vegetable soup, and the adults quiz Evan about life in Pinhurst (hanging out at the Holiday Village or on the recreation ground, depending on the season) and what his plans for New Year's Eve are (hanging out at the Holiday Village). As Auntie Gabs places a bowl of clementines on the table, Jakob says abruptly, "Someone here might be sleeping in a murderer's bed."

I say, "We don't know for sure it was murder."

"Not this again!" says Elaine, tutting.

Evan looks embarrassed and explains about Alice leaving furniture when she sold the house. "I'm pretty sure Dad bought new mattresses, though," he says.

"I don't like this house any more," says Poppy.

Evan doesn't know how to respond so he keeps quiet, his ears turning deep red.

Auntie Gabs inspects the ingredients on a box of biscuits Mum and I brought with a "hmm" and Mum snatches the box out of her hands and says, "For heaven's sake, Gabs, open them. Nobody has to eat them if they don't think the ingredients are up to scratch."

Ivy asks to look at Poppy's row of paper people from

the morning. It transpires she made a mistake, so they are separated as individuals.

"Ah, there are eleven of them. They're *us*?" asks Ivy.

We take a good look at them and try not laugh as we work out who is supposed to be who. I especially like the representation of Steve, with his glasses and gormless expression. She's stuck a skirt on the person who's me with an extra bit of paper even though I've been wearing jeans since I've been here, and given me thick black eyelashes which Tatum says makes me look as if I've been in a fight.

"If you lot clear the table, you can go," says Elaine. "I said I'd make a trifle with Poppy for tonight."

As we finish clearing the table, Baz vomits up something unpleasant from the walk in the middle of the floor, and we are only too happy to leave the kitchen. We run up to the attic.

"I'm going to find that book," says Tatum.

"You reckon?" says Evan. "Game on."

The gloom makes it hard to scan the titles on the book spines. Evan says he'll have to bring a new light bulb next time he comes. At first look it's not there, but Evan finds it after a more thorough search. We were expecting something wide and substantial, not the floppy pamphlet he pulls out triumphantly from between two fat paperbacks.

The cover shows a flowerbed full of different types of daffodil. Not very relevant so far. He flicks through it.

From what we can see there are more black-and-white photos than colour.

"Let's have a look," says Tatum, but Evan holds the book in the air. She tickles him simultaneously in both armpits and he crumples, laughing. The flirting is hard to watch. I look at Ivy and she rolls her eyes.

"Give me a moment," Evan gasps. "I just saw the photo."

Tatum stays right up next to him as he turns the pages hurriedly. "Here." He turns the book outwards and we see a rose garden with a central flowerbed and three borders filled with different roses. The ones in the middle are blood red.

"It's like something from a stately home," says Jakob, whose parents often drag him round historic houses.

We focus our attention on the three figures to the left of the photo. The caption says: *Alice and Doug Billings with their son, John. Their spectacular rose garden is open to the public once a year.* John is in shorts and his legs are podgy. He has white-blond hair and the classic young-kid-trying-to-smile expression. Alice's smile is awkward, as if she's been cajoled into having this photo taken. Doug's arm is curled behind his wife's back, his hand emerging at her waist. Is he steadying her?

Ivy says, "The central flower bed must be where Rose was buried. It's the burial site."

We nod.

"Yes, you're right," breathes Tatum.

"And then she had the garage built there, and destroyed the rose garden in the process," I say.

"Maintaining those roses was probably too much," says Evan. "She wouldn't have wanted anyone helping her, would she? When she sold the house to my dad, she said she wanted everything in the garden to stay the same until she died, and then she didn't mind what he did with it."

"Didn't he think that was odd?" I ask.

Evan shakes his head. "He knew she really loved her garden. I know it's overgrown now in places, but he did his best."

"Are there any more photos of the house?" asks Ivy.

"One more," says Evan. He turns over the page and we see a black-and-white photo of the back lawn, taken from the end of the garden. The caption is: *Peace and tranquillity at Roeshot House*. There are borders bursting with, presumably colourful, flowers. Part of the neat lawn has croquet hoops in it. By the conservatory door there's a stone dragon statue, and along from that is a bench. Alice is sitting on it. The garden looks huge, and so does the house. In contrast, Alice seems small and lonely.

TEN

When Evan leaves, saying if he doesn't his dad will show up and that would be embarrassing, we stay in the attic and Tatum takes photos of the book, then searches the old desk to see if anything could have been left behind from when Alice lived here. Apart from clumps of grey dust, it's empty, as I told her it would be. Clive was bound to have checked the furniture that was left as soon as he took over the house.

I gaze out of the window to the garden at the side of the house. I can see part of the garage from here, sticking out above a tangle of bushes. The window doesn't open far because there's a rusty metal bar in the way, to stop people falling out. The rose garden would have been visible from here. I sit on the window seat and run my fingers over the chipped paint, and random grooves where somebody before me was bored, and scored it with a tool of some kind.

The desk faces a wall and the window is to the right of it. It might not have been in that position when Doug used it up here, but wherever it was, he'd have seen the rose garden when he moved around the room. I sit in the tatty leather swivel chair. It creaks as I turn towards the window. It's hard to imagine Alice burying a body on her own without him even knowing about it. And the story Alice told about Rose going to Switzerland to be a lady's companion – would he have believed that if he didn't know the truth?

The others are immersed in various things. Tatum is reviewing footage on her phone, Ivy's reading a magazine that Mum brought with us, and Jakob is fiddling with his portable speaker.

"Right," says Jakob. "This baby is now *working*. Song requests, anyone, or shall we risk shuffle?"

"Shuffle," I say, going to sit next to him on the sofa.

"OK, now this is boring." Tatum sits upright. "You know what I want to do? See your predictions. The ones you were so cagey about last night. Please?" She makes a pleading face. "*Please.*"

Ivy says, "They'll seem really stupid to you."

"No, they won't. Pleeeeeeease?"

"They're private," I say.

"But I really *really* want to see them," whines Tatum.

Jakob says, "I wish you'd stop going on about them."

"I'm going to keep going on about them until you show me," says Tatum.

"God, Tatum, you're a pain," I say.

"You're really intriguing me now," says Tatum.

"Fine," I snap. I stride to the rug, push it back and lift up the loose floorboard. I see the pile of different pieces of paper. It's my writing on the top sheet. I was the one who wrote down the predictions in the candlelight last year. I freeze.

"Can you smell that?" I ask

The others come closer and it's not just me and my imagination. We can all detect it. Roses.

As I reach in to lift out the paper, dark flakes fall away. I drop it. "Eww."

"Mice droppings?" asks Jakob, crouching beside me.

"No. It was something papery," I say. Ivy shines her phone light and Jakob leans in.

"They're petals. Dried-up petals." He lifts one up by its edge. Is it a *rose petal*?"

"You're playing a joke on me," says Tatum. She has her hand clenched round her phone.

"You're playing a joke on *us*," I say and the other two nod in agreement. "Tell us where you found the rose petals."

"Where would I find rose petals?" she says. "And I didn't know where you kept your predictions in the first place."

I wish she'd cave in and tell us it's a joke. I'd be willing to say on camera that for a while she had us fooled. Anything to stop the prickling of unease.

Tatum starts to film, holding one of the dark red petals in the palm of her spare hand, describing the smell of roses. Her voice is breathy and excited, over the top for the camera . . . but does that mean she's faking?

Next she pulls out the disorganized pile of papers. The sheet on top is what she's looking for. She pauses her commentary. "Oh," she says. "Oh."

I picture the words that I wrote down last year as she reads them out loud:

"Something of great value will be lost
An actual ghost will be seen
Someone in this house will be in a car accident
There will be an unexpected twist of fate
An Amigo will be unlucky in love their whole life
Someone in this house will die."

ELEVEN

"Yup, that's a brutal list," says Tatum.

"You had to be there to understand," says Jakob. "It was because of that book. What does a twist of fate even mean?"

"Things turning out a different way because of something out of our control," I say. I looked up the phrase on the internet a few days after I'd made that prediction. "Maybe that's already happened." I'm thinking of Rose's body being found. Maybe even of Tatum being here with us because of her nan's operation going wrong.

Tatum puts her phone down and looks in the space under the floorboards. "Maybe those petals were always here and you never noticed them."

Jakob shakes his head. "I'd have noticed."

"I know you're going to say it's something to do with Rose's ghost," I say to Tatum. "But it can't be."

Tatum shrugs. "Why can't it be? Give me another explanation if it wasn't any of us."

"Other people staying here might have put them in as a joke. . ." says Ivy.

We're quiet a moment at the thought of people reading our predictions – and then going to the trouble of sourcing rose petals. If that's what happened, it must have been done recently, after the police released the name of the body. Was it someone who'd had too much to drink, who thought it would be funny?

"If might have been Evan," says Tatum.

"No!" I say sharply. "Of course it wasn't."

She laughs. "You're quick to defend him. It's possible." She still has the list in her hand. "Didn't you say you ticked off the predictions if they came true? We had a pen up here, didn't we?" She looks over to the bookshelves where I left the list of *things we know so far*, and the pen.

"Don't!" says Jakob, but it's too late. Tatum's pressed down on the top of the ballpoint pen and she's placed a tick beside: *An actual ghost will be seen.*

I grab the pen from Tatum's hand. "Stop." I snatch the predictions list and other bits of paper from her and shove them back under the floorboards. I replace the loose one and push the rug back into place. Those predictions don't belong to her.

"Don't fool around with them," I say, placing the pen back on the shelves. "It's not funny."

"I'm not fooling around," says Tatum indignantly. She goes to the sofa and drops down on to it. "I think they're interesting. I think something's shifted in this house. It's not a happy place. Can't you feel it too, a sadness in the air?"

Ivy says, "It feels the same as it always does." She's on the floor, leaning against the armchair, shaking a table-tennis ball in her cupped hands.

Jakob says, "It doesn't feel any different to me either."

"But it's never smelled of roses, has it?" asks Tatum, and although the floorboard and the rug are back in place, it still floats in the air, that faint perfume.

"We couldn't get rid of the banana smell for a long time, when you two had that banana fight," says Jakob.

I have an urge to do my ballet stretches, to get rid of the tension in my muscles. I stand up and move my neck and shoulders. Jakob joins in until I do the splits slowly.

"I'm wearing the wrong trousers, sorry," he says. Tatum tuts loudly; she thinks I'm showing off.

"I've had enough of the attic," I say, pushing down on my front leg. "Let's get out of here."

"And do what?" asks Tatum.

"Any ideas, Ivy?" asks Jakob. "You normally come up with something."

"Something fun," I say.

"But not dangerous," says Jakob. He takes off his hat

and shakes his hair. "Ivy persuaded us to go up on the roof the year before last," he says to Tatum, pointing at the skylight. "I screamed the whole time, it was so slippery."

Tatum peers at the skylight. "Look at all those bird droppings," she says, pulling a face.

"Er. . ." Ivy squeezes the side of her mouth, thinking. "We could go down to the bathroom and cut your hair, Jakob?"

"*Or*," says Tatum. "We could give you hair like mine?" She holds up a pink-tipped end. "I've got bleach and dye with me. I was going to give myself a few more sections if I had time. I'll do it for you if you like. If your parents won't have a go at me."

I come out of the splits. I have to admit it would be fun to see Jakob with pink hair. It sounds like a good use of the afternoon.

Jakob's eyes glint with excitement. "I love that idea. Mum and Dad will freak. Obviously. And if school try to exclude me, I can just cut the ends off."

"I want to help," says Ivy.

"You and Leah can keep track of time and keep us company," says Tatum.

"That's big of you," I mutter.

There's plenty of room for four people in the bathroom. Ivy and I settle down next to each other, sitting on towels and leaning against the bath. Tatum clears the glass shelf above the sink of our toothbrushes and toothpastes, and lines up her hair products. Jakob pulls the cord for the double bar heater attached high up on the wall. There's a smell of burning dust and a ticking sound as the metal expands and the bar glows orange. He sets up his speaker on the huge chest of drawers where the clean towels are kept, and once the music's playing, and the room warms up, this starts to feel like a solid Amigo activity.

Tatum sits Jakob on the toilet seat lid and places a towel round his shoulders to protect his clothes. I've never been allowed to dye my hair with anything other than wash-out dye, so I'm not used to the noxious smell of the bleach kit. After arguing about how wide to open the window – toxic fumes versus lowering our core body temperature – Jakob rinses his hair over the bathtub, Ivy and me scrambling out of the way of the showerhead. Tatum sprays deodorant to counteract the smell, which makes us choke, and Ivy throws the window open fully. We cheer when we catch sight of the light ends of Jakob's hair, and Ivy closes the window most of the way.

Next Tatum adds one cream to another to activate the colour, talking us through it as if she's doing an online tutorial.

"D'you think we should have done a spot test first?" asks Jakob as she slops the colour on to the bits of hair that she hasn't pinned up on his head. "In case I have an allergic reaction?"

"Nobody's got time for that," says Tatum. "You'll be fine."

The bathroom door creaks open and for a strange moment, when I can't see anyone there, I think it might be Rose, or Alice, coming to see what we're doing in their house. I hear snuffling, lower my eyes, and see Baz. He isn't his usual exuberant self. His legs are trembly and he's not walking very well. He stands in the middle of the room and coughs.

"What's up, little buddy?" says Ivy.

"Maybe he doesn't like the smell of the products," says Tatum.

Baz coughs again and a couple of specks of blood land on the floor.

"That's serious," says Jakob. "He needs to see a vet."

Ivy uses toilet paper to clean up the mess, then washes her hands and picks him up. "I'll take him down to Mum." She strokes him under his chin and he closes his bloodshot eyes. "Poor thing."

We wait for the pink dye to work, and Ivy comes back telling us that Auntie Gabs is going to keep an eye on Baz, and call the emergency vet if he gets worse. Since Auntie Gabs isn't too worried we all slowly relax, apart from Jakob, who sits on the toilet seat, head up and shoulders back, so the product doesn't drip off. The warmth, steady hum from the heater, and Jakob's chilled playlist are soothing. "This was a good idea," I say.

"Unless I have an allergic reaction, or the colour goes wrong," says Jakob.

"Nothing will go wrong," says Tatum. "I know what I'm doing."

I close my eyes and drift towards sleep. I hear Tatum ask Jakob what the music is and I tune in to the female vocalist, singing a sad, haunting song in a foreign language.

"It's like a soundtrack to a sinister scene in a movie," she says.

Jakob says, "It's Spanish. Something my Spanish teacher played us that I downloaded. D'you like it?"

Tatum says, "No, it's creepy. What's it called?"

I open my eyes and see Jakob walk to the chest of drawers and pick up his phone. He squints at the display. "OK, it translates as... Oh. Oh shit. It translates as 'Crushed Rose'."

The music slows to a strange, high-pitched finish.

"Oh, my God," says Ivy. "Crushed Rose."

Tatum says, "That's *weird*. Perfect soundtrack for my documentary, though."

"It's coincidence," says Jakob.

"We're skipping that if it comes on again," I say.

Jakob's high-pitched phone alarm pierces through the conversation. "Time to see the transformation," he says.

We watch him kneel on the mat at the side of the bath. Tatum helps him rinse off the thick gloop and conditions his hair with another tube of product. The ends of his hair have definitely changed colour, but we can't see quite how much until Tatum finds the hairdryer in the chest of drawers and the warm air from it gradually reveals the brightness. She won't let him look in the mirror until his hair is dry but he grins as we applaud.

Eventually Tatum leads him over to the mirror above the sink.

He runs his hands through his hair. "Oh, wow. That's. . ." He turns sideways. "Wow."

Tatum takes a photo of the back of his head, and he enlarges it.

"Fan. Tas. Tic," he murmurs. "Mum and Dad are going to *love* it!"

We laugh.

"Fake tan next?" asks Tatum, waving a bottle from her enormous wash-kit bag.

"I'll pass, thanks," says Jakob.

"You name it, I've got it," says Tatum. She holds up a foundation. "This is so nice. It blends really easily. And look at my smoky eyes palette. Anyone want to be made-over?"

"Me," I say. "I'd like smoky eyes."

"Sure. Sit on the side of the bath then," orders Tatum.

Ivy goes to see if Poppy wants to come up and join in.

It doesn't take long for Tatum to do my eyes. Jakob stands next to her, watching how she does it. When she's finished she says, "Your turn next, Jakob. Take a seat."

"What?" says Jakob, but he sits.

"I'm going to make you look fabulous," says Tatum. She reaches for her foundation and presses on the pump so that a tiny bit comes out on to her finger.

I hold my breath as she smooths the foundation on. Jakob is transforming into someone else. He agrees to contouring, and blusher. He tenses his lips for the lip liner. I select a reddish-brown lipstick from Tatum's wash kit and she fills in his lips.

We've braided his hair before, and plucked his eyebrows, and he's been happy to let us pamper him, but this is a step further than we've ever gone. He's loving it. We laugh when he says he doesn't suit that shade of lipstick and asks Tatum for something more pink. He blots the first layer with a sheet of toilet paper, and waits for Tatum to brush in a second layer.

"You've done theatre things, haven't you?" says Tatum. "You're used to wearing make-up."

Jakob nods, but he's only ever talked about being in one production.

"Smoky eyes next," says Tatum. I watch intently so I learn what to do.

"Ivy's not going to recognize you by the time she comes back," I say.

"That gives me an idea," says Tatum. She quickly finishes off his eyes, and releases him to look at himself in the mirror above the sink.

He stares at himself before saying, "Who even am I?"

"You can be my younger sister," says Tatum. "Want to borrow some clothes? We already have matching hair." She squeezes his shoulders when he makes a reluctant face. "Go on! You're taller than me but kind of the same size otherwise. Come and see what I've got."

Apart from jeans and leggings, Tatum's brought a dress

and fake leather miniskirt with her. She holds up the skirt and says, "You know you want to."

Jakob looks at me. I can't interpret that look. "All right," he says after a slight pause. "Have you got tights or am I going to have to shave my legs?"

"Awesome," says Tatum. She throws a pair of silvery tights and a black crop top at him and says we'll meet him back in the bathroom.

He knocks on the door when he's ready. Tatum flings it open and says, "Well, look at you!"

He looks stunning. Strangely himself, but also not. "D'you like the new me?" he asks, standing side on and raising an eyebrow.

I laugh. "Of course!" I stop laughing, suddenly aware in that split second of the weight of the moment. This doesn't feel like a joke, not really. "Of course I do. And you need heels."

Ivy comes running in telling us Poppy doesn't want to come upstairs, and stops dead. "Jakob? Oh, my God. Jakob?" She circles round him. "You look *incredible!*"

His feet are too big for Tatum's heels and neither Ivy nor I brought any. He just about manages to fit into Ivy's fluffy slides

We take endless photos while he poses, and complains the skirt's too tight round the waist.

"Does anyone have make-up wipes?" asks Jakob.

Tatum nods. "But I dare you to go down to dinner like that. What d'you think? Are you brave enough?"

"I'd choose the wipes," I say.

"Bet you anything, your mum's first question is 'Have you done your violin practice?'" says Ivy. "But seriously, she'll flip out."

"It'll be hilarious," says Jakob. The gong sounds downstairs. We've been in the bathroom much longer than we realized.

Jakob picks up his hat from the chest of drawers. He knows he's got time to wipe off the make-up and change if he hurries, and his hat can hide the pink ends until he's ready to show them. "You know what?" he says, putting the hat down, "Let's do this."

TWELVE

We tumble down from the attic, laughing at Jakob in the skirt because he can hardly walk in it, and the slides are too small. We pass two mirrors and he admires his face in each one. Outside the kitchen, he stops.

We have the giggles now. "Your mascara's smudged. Let me sort it," whispers Tatum. She wipes her finger under his eye, and he squirms. "Ow."

"Looking fabulous!" says Tatum, and she pulls him into the kitchen, saying, "Look who we've brought with us!"

"It's Jakob!" exclaims Poppy, who is sitting at the table with Steve. She stares at him, then to the adults to gauge their reaction.

Auntie Gabs is placing a bowl of rice on the table. She

lets it drop the last little bit so it wobbles for a second, threatening to tip over.

Mum is right behind her with green beans. She gives us a proper reaction. "Oh, Jakob. You look … what a transformation!"

His parents are by the oven. "What's going on?" says Marc. He's frowning.

"Let me introduce my sister, Jane," says Tatum, with a large grin.

She's pitching it so wrong. I shrivel with awkwardness by the fridge.

"We just picked Jane up from the coach," continues Tatum. "She's doing a little holiday swap with your son, Jakob. She'll be with us for dinner. Please make her feel welcome." She opens her arm in a theatrical gesture. "Jane, please meet Jakob's parents. They aren't normally lost for words." Finally she stops.

"Ta-da!" says Jakob. His voice is too small. The air has thinned.

"Is this a dare?" asks Elaine.

"I guess so," says Jakob.

"You look absurd," says Marc.

Elaine's face is tight. "D'you want to explain this, Jakob?"

"It's funny – don't you think it's funny?" says Jakob.

Before she can reply, Marc says coldly. "Go upstairs and sort yourself out."

"Sort myself out?" says Jakob.

"Just go!" roars Marc.

Jakob goes, his cheeks bright with more than blusher.

Elaine fixes her gaze on Tatum. "I presume you're responsible for that dye. Is it permanent?"

"Er, yes. But he can cut the ends off if his school gives him grief."

Steve, who has blended into the background until now, says, "It's a creative way to spend the afternoon, I suppose." Master of the unhelpful comment.

Elaine glares at him.

"Count yourself lucky you don't have children," says Marc. "Especially a teenager."

Steve reels slightly, and takes his glasses off and polishes them with the bottom of his sweatshirt.

Auntie Gabs clears her throat. "Come on, you two, you'll be laughing about this next year. There are far bigger things to worry about." *Like your husband dying and your kid being ill* is what she probably means, except she's more considerate of Elaine's feelings.

"I like a joke, Gabs," says Marc. "But that was pushing things too far."

We eat stiffly. Gabs thanks Steve for driving all the way to the supermarket in Riddingham for the chillies for the Thai fishcakes. She doesn't know how she managed to forget them. The adults talk about a drama series from years ago. Poppy draws a zigzag design on the inside of her wrist in felt-tip pen and tells us that she's going to have a tattoo as soon as she can.

"Eighteen," says Ivy.

Poppy says, "I'll make my own until then."

We wait for Jakob to reappear, but he doesn't. As we stack our plates and Mum assembles pudding for the next course, out of meringue, cream and strawberries, I suggest taking up some food for him.

"Leave him, Leah," says Marc.

Someone needs to tell him it should be OK for Jakob to experiment like that. I wish Tatum hadn't made it into something so awkward. Or pushed it so far.

Mum places dessert on the table.

"That looks good," says Steve.

Mum smiles. "Before you ask, Gabs, no I didn't make the meringues."

"Where's Baz?" asks Poppy.

"Asleep in the lounge," says Auntie Gabs.

"I heard he ate something on the walk," says Marc.

Auntie Gabs sighs. "I've got him under observation. I'll have to take him to the vet tomorrow if he's still not well."

As we clear the table, Tatum whispers that Jakob should have stood up for himself better.

"He wouldn't have wanted a massive row," I whisper back, but I wonder if she's right.

"What does everyone want to do this evening?" asks Auntie Gabs. She sounds tired.

Elaine pours herself another glass of wine from the bottle that's been cleared away to the counter. "Quick game of cards, Gabs? Then I'll take a sandwich up to Jakob."

"Mum, Baz isn't in the lounge," says Poppy.

"Oh," says Auntie Gabs. "Did anyone let him outside?"

"He might have got out when I went to get more wood for the fire," says Steve. He goes to open the back door and calls for him. He uses the wrong intonation – it's too polite.

"I'll go and find him," says Auntie Gabs. "Poppy, go and do your teeth and get into bed. You had a late night yesterday, so it's early to bed this evening."

"Are you sleeping upstairs or downstairs?" asks Ivy.

"Downstairs," says Poppy.

"Sure?" I say. I don't want to remind her about her nightmare, but surely sleeping in the same room as Ivy would be better.

"I like the little lounge," says Poppy.

"All right," says Ivy, "but call *me* on the walkie-talkie if you need anything. Mum needs her sleep." To Elaine, she says, "We'll skip the cards and go upstairs."

As we leave the kitchen, Ivy points to her hoodie pocket and whispers to me, "Biscuits and sweets for Jakob."

Jakob is lying on his bed, changed into his tracksuit bottoms and a T-shirt, his face clear of make-up, his pink-tipped hair mesmerizing. "Hi," he says without enthusiasm. "That didn't go so well, did it?"

"Forget about it," I say, sitting on his bed. "We're here to cheer you up."

Ivy empties her pocket and Jakob perks up. He unwraps a chocolate and shoves it into his mouth.

"Your mum's bringing up a sandwich soon," Ivy says and apologizes for us having persuaded him to go downstairs dressed as a girl.

Strictly speaking, it was Tatum who dared him.

Tatum picks up the can of hair mousse on his bedside table and says, "This brand's rubbish. You need to up your game now your hair is more out there." She wanders over to the music stand in the corner of the room, next to his closed violin case, and thumbs through the music. "Being able to read music must be cool."

Jakob shrugs and sits up. His nose is reddish, as if he might have been crying. "My dad does my head in. He goes on about things being appropriate or inappropriate. Like who is he to decide that?"

I scooch further on to the bed to make room for the other two. "Sorry to break it to you, Jakob, but your dad is nowhere near as annoying as Steve. Have you seen his polishing-the-glasses routine? He's always pushing them up his nose too. Why doesn't he go to an optician and get them tightened if they keep slipping down? And have you heard him grunt when he sits down?"

Ivy's laughing.

"I could go on," I say.

"Go on," she says.

"He's always losing his effing binoculars. He can have whole conversations about those binoculars. About the high-spec optics. How they were some big present from his dad back in the day."

"I don't know," says Tatum. "Steve doesn't seem too bad to me." She pulls a face as if something's just occurred to her. "Obsessed with binoculars, though? Like, *how* obsessed? He doesn't look out of the window with them when you're sunbathing or anything like that, does he?"

I recoil. "No. He's weird enough without any of that stuff. He rubs his bald patch like this. Have you seen him do that? And when he concentrates his mouth is open like this." I do an impression.

"You do this when you're concentrating, Leah," says Ivy. She gently chews the inside of her lip.

Jakob sits up. "You're so right, Ivy! She does."

I do it, and they laugh.

It makes me laugh too.

Tatum has zoned out of the conversation. She's trying to find a signal on her phone. I don't know why she bothers. We've tried before in every inch of our bedrooms, and we've told her that.

There's a knock on the door, and we shout, "Come in!"

Tatum calls, "Is it room service?"

Elaine comes in with a tray – there are two sandwiches and a glass of milk. The sandwich is surrounded by cut-up chunks of tomato and cucumber. "Ooh, salad garnish too," says Tatum, but Ivy and I don't laugh because we don't want to antagonize Elaine. When she's in a mood, she can be scary. She looks as if she has something to say, but it's not what we expect.

"Baz didn't come up here, did he?" Elaine asks with a

frown. "He's not coming when he's called. Gabs is really worried about him."

"I'm going to look for him," says Ivy.

"I'll come," I say.

"Outside?" says Tatum. "Yes, me too. You can join us when you've eaten your sandwich, Jakob."

Elaine comes downstairs with us. Mum and Steve are putting their coats on.

"Baz doesn't normally run off, does he?" asks Mum.

Ivy shakes her head. "Only if he's chasing a squirrel or something."

"He was wobbly when he was upstairs earlier," I say. "All the coughing and little splatters of blood. Not his usual self at all." My stomach is balled-up with the worry I see on everyone's faces.

As we step outside we hear Gabs calling Baz's name over and over down at the bottom of the drive. Marc appears down the side of the house. "No sign of him in the back garden," he says. "He must have gone out of the gate."

We walk down the drive as Marc explains how we can split up and look for Baz in the surrounding roads.

Tatum stops walking and looks at a little heap of clothing next to the bins – then moves away to be sick into a bush.

Ivy and I go closer and see it's not clothing at all.

It's Baz.

His head is smashed in, jaw open, swollen tongue split. His bloodied body is stiff with death.

We scream at exactly the same time.

THIRTEEN

We huddle together in the lounge, apart from Poppy, who's already asleep in the little lounge, and nobody wants to think about how she'll react when she's told the news. Jakob has come downstairs and I was the one who had to tell him the news. Ivy cries uncontrollably on the sofa between Auntie Gabs and Elaine; I've never seen her like this before, and I hate that nothing any of us says can calm her down. Eventually she cries herself into a stupor, and clutches her head, saying she needs painkillers, which Elaine fetches.

"We'll report the hit-and-run to the police tomorrow," says Marc. "Cars go through the village at quite a speed."

"Baz must have tried to get back to us and only made it

as far as the bins," says Elaine. She puts her hand over her mouth. The thought of Baz dying on his own by the bins is horrific.

"They'd have to have known they'd hit something," says Auntie Gabs. "Despicable not to stop." She shakes her head. "I don't think Baz was himself when he went out of the gate. Perhaps he collapsed before he was run over. But the person still should have stopped." She lets out a sob.

"I've covered his body," says Marc. "I'll speak to Clive in the morning. See if he minds us burying him, or whether he'd rather we took him somewhere for, erm, disposal."

"As long as he doesn't go where Rose Strathmortimer was buried," says Tatum.

All three Amigos glare at her. Does she say those stupid things on purpose, or does she never think before she speaks? It's like she's enjoying this.

The temperature in the room is falling. The adults have let the fire die down, and the heating must have gone off. I'm so tired, but every time I close my eyes I see Baz, his grotesquely damaged body and his fur matted with blood.

"Why don't we have some more tea or hot chocolate?" suggests Auntie Gabs.

"I'll make tea," I say.

Mum follows me into the kitchen where I cry into a folded tea towel. I didn't think I had any more tears left. Mum hugs me. The weight of her arms and the smell of her are so familiar and comforting that I'm still for a moment.

"I won't go away tomorrow if you don't want me to," she says softly.

I move away to get some kitchen roll for my nose. "No, you should go," I say. I don't want to be around Steve.

I wake from a restless sleep to the sound of Poppy shouting and crying, and I look across at Tatum, who winces from her bed. Wordlessly, we decide to stay in bed longer.

A while later there's a knock at the door, and Jakob comes in with his duvet round his shoulders.

I can't stop looking at his pink-tipped hair.

"Did you hear the car?" he asks. "Clive's here. He's burying Baz in the back garden with Gabs and Poppy. I knocked on Ivy's door to see if she was OK, but there was no answer. D'you think we should check on her?"

I scramble out of bed. Ivy's not in her room. I run downstairs and find her in the kitchen sitting at the table, gazing at a mug of tea. The lights are off. She gives me a half-smile. "I know they're outside burying Baz, but I've already said goodbye to him. I don't need to watch him being buried."

"I understand," I say. I look down at my T-shirt, leggings and bare feet, and wish I'd spent a couple of seconds layering up.

"Put your coat on if you're cold," suggests Ivy.

We wore our coats up to bed last night because the house was so cold. The only one here on the hooks by the back door is Steve's. It smells of his horrible aftershave and

I can't bring myself to put it on, so I go into the lounge for a blanket to drape over me. The room is freezing and I've never really noticed how dark and heavy the furniture is in here.

Back in the kitchen, Ivy's been joined by Jakob and Tatum, and Steve is looking around for his binoculars. Again.

"I've looked everywhere," he mutters. "I'm not sure when I last had them. Perhaps it was. . ."

There are noises by the back door, and Clive, Auntie Gabs and Poppy trudge in, bringing air that slices through us. Ivy gets up and goes to hug Poppy, who, standing there in her skinny jeans, appears more frail than ever. Her face is puffy from crying.

"I'm so sorry about Baz," I say to her.

"He was the best dog ever," sobs Poppy, putting her hands out to steady herself on a chair. She sits down. "He was, like, my only friend."

I exchange glances with Jakob. I don't know what to say.

"He was lucky to have you," says Jakob. "He had a nice life with you." He places his arm round her shoulder and gives her a mini hug so as not to hurt her.

"Thanks for offering to help me dig the hole," Clive says to Steve. "I thought there was an old coal shovel in the garage, but I could only find the gardening spade."

Steve nods. I think to myself, *if he was the one to let Baz out, he should have dug the hole himself.*

Mum appears at the back door with some scissors and twigs with little yellow flowers. "I thought we could put some winter jasmine in a jam jar for Baz's grave."

"That's nice," says Auntie Gabs. "But Elaine and Marc have gone into Riddingham to buy a plant to mark the grave. You'll have a cup of tea with us, won't you, Clive?"

"All right," he says. "A quick one. Thanks." He asks if he can wash his hands, then sits down on a chair, groaning as he does. Somehow it's not as annoying as when Steve does his sitting-down grunt. "Stiff back," Clive says. "Not been right for a couple of months, since some idiot swung into this drive too fast, not expecting me and my van to be there. It could have been really nasty, the speed he was going."

"Car accident?" asks Tatum. She looks at us, her eyes knowing.

Someone in this house will be in a car accident, she mouths. I pray she doesn't say anything out loud.

Mum says something about physiotherapy and Jakob motions we should go up to the attic. Poppy has taken the twigs from Mum and is carefully arranging them in a glass tumbler. She doesn't need us right now.

The four of us slide out of the room. As soon as we're in the attic, Tatum takes out her phone and says, "We should discuss this on camera."

"For God's sake," I say, but we're all talking over each other, so I let her get on with it. She'll have rubbish footage.

The prediction was "Someone in this house will be in a car accident". Clive wasn't in the house when the prediction was made.

But he was in a car accident on the grounds. How likely is that?

He's connected to the house. He owns it.

Maybe he WAS in the house when we did the predictions. He might have dropped something round when we were in the attic and we didn't know.

How long do predictions last? For the year? Or longer?

You've got to admit it's creepy.

Ivy holds her hand up to shut us up. "What about 'Someone in this house will die'? Do you think that's Baz? I know he's not a person but he was a member of the family. When Poppy was little she told her teacher that she had a brother called Baz."

"A dog's not the same as a person," says Tatum. She holds her phone steady as she films. "No, I think we can only tick off the car accident."

FOURTEEN

Mum calls us from the bottom of the stairs. "Leah, Steve and I are going now."

I race downstairs, still with the blanket round my shoulders. I say a brief "Bye then" to Steve, but I give Mum a big hug. Maybe a couple of intense days with Steve will make her see sense.

"Call us if you need us, won't you?" says Steve. He sounds hesitant. "Look after yourself. Oh, and keep an eye out for my binoculars."

"Yeah, yeah," I say.

"I have a message from Clive," says Mum. "He said to tell you Evan's coming round at eleven."

"What's the time now?" I ask. I haven't had a shower. I smell of sweat and old blanket.

"Ten to," says Steve.

I don't bother to wave them off. I rush upstairs and yell the news to the others and call shotgun on the shower.

When Evan arrives a bit after eleven, the four of us are downstairs and dressed, though my hair is wet and I've forgotten to put concealer on the spot that can't decide whether or not to erupt on my chin. He walks through the back door cautiously after Ivy's opened it, as if he's not sure how we'll be. He knows about Baz; he says how sorry he is.

Poppy starts crying and Auntie Gabs takes her into the lounge to watch TV.

"Now I feel really bad. I didn't mean to make it worse," says Evan.

"You haven't," says Ivy. "We're still in shock, that's all."

Evan nods. He doesn't look as if he's spent much time on his hair this morning either, but it looks good veering off in different directions. There are three cute little moles on his cheek. I imagine joining them up with my finger. "We better go, if you still want to," he says. "Donna said quarter past eleven was a good time if we wanted to call and talk to her about Alice Billings. But I understand if you're not up for it. . ."

"Really?" says Tatum. "Donna's agreed to talk to us? That's fantastic!" She adds in a more subdued way, "It'll help us take our minds off Baz."

We scrabble to put on shoes and get out of the door. Ivy scribbles a quick note for the adults on the back of a photocopied recipe her mum's left on the counter. My head hurts as we walk down the side passage, doing up our coats, because my hair is wet and the wind is cold.

Tatum insists on filming us, telling us she needs filler shots for the documentary. I bat her away.

"Oh, come on, you guys being in shot is really going to add authenticity," she cajoles.

Jakob fiddles with his hat, and Ivy says she can't walk normally when there's a camera on her.

"I'm going to have to get you to walk down the driveway again," says Tatum, and only shuts up when Evan tells her there's no time, we're already late for Donna.

"By the way," he says, when we're walking along the pavement, "Mum knows we're going to Donna's, but Dad thinks I'm hanging out with you to make sure everyone's OK after, y'know, Baz."

"Which you are," says Tatum. "You're doing a great job."

Donna's house is in a wide road of neat bungalows, some with an upper floor bolted on. Hers is the only one with a purple front door. She opens it, wearing a purple jumper and jeans, and mini dreamcatcher earrings. "Hello, my precious," she says to Evan and grabs him for a hug. "You're usually out when I'm round at yours. Nice to see you. Had a good Christmas?"

Evan nods and tells her his mum sends her love.

After we've taken off our shoes and left our coats on a chair, Donna ushers us into her tidy, narrow kitchen. She asks us how our holiday's going (we answer politely), if Evan's mum got the coat she'd been dropping hints about all December (she did), and if Evan's sister is still going out with the boy who can juggle knives (we stare at Evan). We stand around while the kettle boils, and Donna makes us tea and un-sellotapes a tin of Christmas biscuits.

"Help yourselves," she says and we dive on the corrugated packaging printed with the biscuit descriptions. "Go down to the bottom layer, if you want."

Donna takes us through to the lounge. There are purple curtains and a large silver Christmas tree. Ivy, Jakob, Tatum and I squash on to the sofa, leaving the two armchairs for Evan and Donna.

Donna places both her hands round her mug. "I don't want to say anything I shouldn't about Alice, but you're not journalists and you're staying in her old house so I say, fair enough. I'd want to know what the hell was going on too."

Pressed up so close to Tatum on the sofa, I'm aware of her reaching into the pocket of her hoodie, and I wonder if she's recording this conversation on her phone.

"As Evan must have told you, I wasn't in Alice's room when she told matron about the body in the garden," says Donna. "But I did know Alice, and she was quite agitated in her last few days. Matron said she was calm after she'd confessed, but at the time she didn't know if Alice was hallucinating or if it was real. Of course, if she'd known Alice was going to die so soon afterwards, she'd have asked her lots of questions."

"D'you think Alice murdered her sister?" asks Tatum.

Donna is taken aback by Tatum's directness but she must have been anticipating the question. "Oooh, I can't say," she says. "You think you know someone but then they turn out not to be the person you thought they were, if you get my drift. But before I heard about the body I'd have said she was a kind, sweet-natured lady. That's what everyone said at the funeral. Her son John was in total shock."

"So Alice didn't say anything else at all?" asks Jakob.

Donna takes a gulp of tea. "She said something about how she was ashamed, but it was rambling and didn't make sense to Matron. It was a good job Matron reported it to the police, though, wasn't it?"

"Did she know exactly where in the garden Rose had been buried?" asks Tatum. She's definitely speaking in her filming voice.

"Yes, I believe so," says Donna.

This seems the wrong conversation to be having in a room with a silver tree and a frog ornament on the mantelpiece with a Santa hat, holding a sign that says *Ho Ho Hoppy Holidays!*

"Have you heard anything about how Rose died?" asks Ivy.

Donna shakes her head. "No, not yet. But if people can tell what a Stone Age man died from, they'll know what happened to that poor wee girl."

"My little sister says she saw Alice's ghost," says Ivy.

"The house has a really weird vibe," says Tatum.

"You're only saying that because you know the body was found in the garden," says Evan.

"As soon as I stepped into the house, I felt it," says Tatum.

Donna's flustered. "Evan says you stay at Rocshot House every year. It's nice you feel so connected to it."

"We should organize a memorial for Rose," says Ivy. "Some way for her to be remembered."

We look at each other. It's an inspired idea, and we voice our agreement loudly.

Donna smiles. "That sounds lovely. I tell you who knew Rose, Evan. Your old violin teacher, Margery. They were school friends. She came to visit Alice regularly at Silverways."

"You play the violin too?" asks Jakob.

"Lol. I can't wait to hear you two play a duet together," says Tatum. She's lost the filming voice.

Evan is horrified. "No! They made everyone do a year of violin when we were nine. Somebody gave them money and a pile of violins. It was the worst thing ever."

Donna laughs. "Margery was very strict. My son Fraser was petrified of her. He's grown up now, but he says she was his scariest teacher."

"I used to pretend to be ill on violin days," says Evan.

"So Margery would know if the sisters got on?" Tatum asks.

"Yes, she would," says Donna. "But I'm sure she didn't know anything about Rose's death. She's not the sort of person to keep quiet about a thing like that."

"D'you think Margery would talk to us?" asks Tatum. I can't believe she'd ask, but I admire her boldness. Why would Margery speak to us? I look at Evan to see what he thinks of the idea, and he's wincing.

"She'd like to see Evan, I'm sure," says Donna, smiling at his expression. "If you explained about a possible memorial she might like to be involved with that. I suppose she *might* like to talk about Alice with you, especially since you know her old house so well."

"Wait until Dad hears about a memorial," says Evan. "He'll go mad."

"Evan, he's only being jittery about bookings," says Donna. "This thing will be old news soon enough. A discreet memorial of some kind, something that doesn't put off the punters, is what you need."

"Or your dad could go big with the memorial and offer ghost tours," says Tatum. "I've heard haunted houses can make a lot of money."

Evan frowns at her.

"I'll phone Margery later and see if she'll talk to you," says Donna, "but you'd have to tread carefully."

FIFTEEN

"Tatum, you should have asked Donna if she minded being recorded," I say when we're outside on the pavement.

"It was only audio, and I'll use snippets, not the whole thing," says Tatum.

Evan says, "She's a family friend. She's done us a favour. Don't get her into trouble."

Tatum glares at me for being a snitch. I like the way Evan says "us", though.

"Donna can be an anonymous source," says Tatum.

"You could get someone else to say her words," says Ivy. "And film their silhouette."

"This project's actually so cool now we've got into it,"

says Jakob. He pulls a what-are-you-looking-at-me-like-that-for face at me. "Just saying," he mutters.

An older girl walks towards us with a dog on a lead. Ivy looks away and none of us mention Baz, but I think of his body in the cold ground.

"Can I do any more filming in Pinhurst?" asks Tatum when the dog has gone past, and the girl has tipped her head back briefly as a hi to Evan. "Places we know Alice went to."

"I could show you Silverways, the care home?" says Evan. "It's not far from here."

I'm curious to see it. Each link with Alice makes her feel more real. We walk slowly, with Evan giving a running commentary, taking in the village in a way we've never done before. The primary school where Evan had his violin lessons and once threw a conker at a passer-by who complained so Evan was made to go round to his house with his parents to apologize. The hall where Alice organized Christmas craft fairs in aid of charity. The park where Evan's sister's best friend's cousin was caught dealing. The bus shelter where Evan asked out his ex-girlfriend Holly.

"Tell us more about Holly," says Ivy, giving me a sly glance.

"We went out for about six months, until she dumped me at Halloween," says Evan. "Don't worry, I'm over it."

"Ahh, that's good," says Tatum. "I recently split up with my boyfriend. We'd been going out for a year and a half. It had to happen, though."

As if anyone cares. But Evan asks her about her ex-boyfriend, and we have to listen to her tell us he couldn't believe his luck when she got with him.

A car horn beeps behind us and someone yells out of a window. "Evaaaaaaaan! See you tonight, yeah?"

Evan waves. When the car's moved on, he says, "Hey, what are you guys doing tonight for New Year's Eve? You want to come to the Holiday Village? There's a disco on at nine, until one. I can get you in for free – I know most of the people behind the bar."

"Our parents wouldn't let us," says Ivy.

"We could ask," says Tatum. "Come on. We're old enough to go out, and they know Evan. Sort of."

"Me and a few of my mates would be walking back your way," says Evan. "See what they say."

"Sounds fun," says Jakob.

"That's Silverways," says Evan. "That building there."

Tatum holds her phone up to film. The care home is a large house set back from the road, with six car park spaces in front of it. I assumed we'd stay on the pavement to gawp, but Tatum beckons us on to the path that leads to the glass front porch. I'm right behind her so I see she's zooming in on the multiple signage on the porch. *Deliveries at side entrance. No junk mail. All visitors to sign in. Maple Care Ltd.* She can't capture the lunch smell: boiled meat and stewed vegetables.

"I'll pretend I'm Alice's granddaughter, if you like," she says. "Get some quality info." She places her phone in her pocket. "Don't panic, I'm not recording."

Evan rushes after her. "They won't believe you. If there was a granddaughter they'd know about her."

Tatum looks at him and presses the buzzer by the porch door with a defiant grin.

A woman with cropped grey hair in a navy blue uniform opens the front door and steps into the porch area to open the glass door. "Hello," she says with professional cheer, which ebbs when she sees there are five of us. "If you're here to ask about weekend jobs or volunteering, you'll need to hand in a CV." There is a nicer smell of fresh laundry now the front door is open. I see grey flooring and some pigeonholes for post.

"Thanks," says Evan hurriedly. "Sorry to bother you."

"I'm..." says Tatum, but she doesn't have the nerve to follow it through.

Jakob giggles nervously.

"She's looking for a brochure," I say, because I'm embarrassed this care worker thinks we're mucking around, and even if she doesn't know Evan, she probably knows one of his relatives. "We're doing a social care project ... for geography."

"Oh. OK. Let me think. We do have one somewhere," says the woman. "Stay there." She leaves the porch door open and closes the front door behind her as she goes back into the building.

"Good save," says Ivy.

I step into the porch, trying to imagine myself in Alice's shoes. She must have lived in fear of her sister's body being discovered after she left Roeshot House. Was she tempted to change her name and leave the village? As she got to the end of her own life, did she think more and more about her sister, and the life that was cut short? Did she see ghosts too?

Jakob asks me what the hell I think I'm doing.

There's a shelf with a large, sprawling spider plant. Underneath it are some plastic gardening clogs and a container of bird-friendly slug pellets. There's a recycling bag, two-thirds full of flyers about takeway deliveries, window cleaning and decorating. On the inside of the door there are more signs. *Stop! Is the front door secure? Do not give the entry code to anyone without checking first with Brenda. Mrs Lupin is NOT allowed out on her own. Mr Brooks, remember your inhaler!!!*

I wonder if Alice was friends with Mr Brooks or Mrs Lupin, if she got on with Brenda. As I step out of the porch, the front door swings open and the nurse-person hands a square brochure to Tatum. There's a circular stain on the front from a cup of tea or coffee. "Good luck with your project," she adds, kindly, before closing the door.

We walk slowly back to Roeshot House. Tatum flips through the brochure. "Just think," she says, "this could have been where Alice made her deathbed confession!" She holds up a photo of an unoccupied bedroom, with a blue cover on a single bed, a sink, wardrobe and chest of drawers.

"We're not sure it was a confession yet," says Evan.

"She confessed she knew her sister was buried in her old garden," says Tatum. "So it's a confession."

Ivy takes the brochure from her for a closer look. "It says there are nine bedrooms, so that's a one-in-nine chance of it being Alice's room."

Jakob tells Tatum to take a photo of the bedroom for the documentary. Nobody's much interested in the brochure after that so I take it and look at photos of the residents' lounge, the dining room and the garden.

When I look up, Evan is walking beside me. "Something's been puzzling me," he says, his voice low, glancing up at the others ahead. "Dad and I tried to work out where Baz was hit by the car, but we couldn't find any blood. And no tyre marks. Baz had to walk a long way up the drive to the bins with severe injuries, didn't he?"

I frown. "So? What does that mean?"

"Nothing, really. Just . . . he couldn't have been run over accidentally by one of your cars, could he?" he says as if he's embarrassed to mention it out loud, but I realize it's a valid question.

"I'm not sure anyone went out in the car yesterday. We did the Chandler's Hill walk, and then. . ." I think back. No one's quite sure when Baz was last seen.

"Hey!" I call to the others. "Random question, but do you remember if anyone went anywhere in the car yesterday?"

Jakob and Tatum shake their heads.

"Erm, didn't Steve go and buy chillies in Riddingham?" asks Ivy. "Why? What's the matter?"

I swear. Jakob, Ivy and Tatum wait for Evan and me to catch up with them, wanting an explanation.

"Steve could have run Baz over, then pretended he'd let him out of the door by mistake, letting us think Baz was run over on the road – not by him," I say. I stare at the road, anger pulsing in my head.

"Oh, God, that's so upsetting," says Jakob.

"If it was him, he'd have known," says Evan, nodding. "You can't hit a dog and not realize." He sees our appalled faces. "But I'm not accusing anyone. It occurred to me, that's all. An alternative explanation."

"And now Steve's gone away so we can't check the car," says Ivy.

"We'll do it as soon as he and Mum get back," I say.

SIXTEEN

At lunch, Tatum asks if she, Ivy, Jakob and I can go to the Holiday Village disco.

"On New Year's Eve?" says Elaine. "Out of the question. We should all be together."

"It would be fun," I say. "And we can't be all together anyway because Mum and Steve aren't here." Saying Steve's name out loud makes me feel queasy.

"They're getting older now, Elaine," says Auntie Gabs. "We wouldn't have wanted to be with our parents at their age, would we?"

"My parents let me go out last New Year's Eve," says Tatum. "It wasn't a big deal."

Elaine is pushing her lips together tightly. It's not a good sign.

"We've already spent lots of time all together," says Ivy. "We'd go at nine or ten, after Poppy's gone to bed. We wouldn't be gone the whole evening."

"But you'd be gone for midnight?" says Elaine.

Tatum says, "That's the idea, yes. The disco finishes at one, and Evan and some friends will be walking back this way."

Poppy's drawing a pattern on the palm of her hand with a biro. "I don't mind if you go."

"Are you sure?" asks Ivy. "I can stay behind if you prefer."

Poppy shakes her head. "No, I'll be fine. I'll probably be asleep by then anyway."

"I suppose if they're sensible. . ." Marc says to Elaine.

"To be honest, I'm feeling so tired, I'm not sure I'll make it to midnight," says Gabs.

"Well, Marc and I will have to stay up, then, and check they're all home safe and sound," says Elaine.

We give triumphant looks to each other, but keep a lid on our excitement.

"Cool," says Tatum.

"What are you doing to your hand, Poppy?" mutters Elaine.

"Making it look nice," says Poppy. She pushes her plate away. It still has most of her lunch on it.

"What d'you want to do this afternoon?" I ask Poppy. "We could go to the rec, where the swings are?"

Poppy shakes her head. "It's too far, and I don't want to go there without Baz."

"Jewellery-making?" suggests Ivy.

"Yes — you've got your jewellery kit," says Gabs.

Ivy goes to fetch it from Poppy's bag. It consists of silver wire, silver beads, china beads, clasps, earring hooks, and a small pair of pliers. We make jewellery for Poppy, while she creates little spiral decorations from the wire to attach to the necklace Jakob's making. I ask to measure her wrist for a bracelet and she holds out her thin arm. She likes the dangly earrings Tatum makes best. She doesn't have her ears pierced yet, so she wraps them in kitchen towel and places them in her pencil case.

I tell her to be careful not to stab herself with them, and she says, "I could stab someone else if I wanted."

Jakob catches my eye. We're the only ones to have heard her because Tatum and Ivy are arguing about how to attach a clasp.

"You wouldn't want to do that," he says.

She acts as if she hasn't heard.

We finish up the jewellery, and she wears the necklace, bracelet and anklet to show the adults, who are talking about plans for the week. Poppy curls up next to her mum on the sofa, and Ivy takes the kit back to the little lounge and comes back with Poppy's pillow.

"Thank you, darling Ivy," says Auntie Gabs. "You teenagers go and have some time to yourselves."

In the attic we discuss what the dress code for the disco might be. We decide it doesn't really matter because Tatum is the only one who's brought something appropriate, and we'll just have to make the best of what we've got. Tatum jokes that Jakob can borrow her skirt again and I tell her to shut up, and he gives me a look which tells me he didn't want me to wade in like that.

He removes "Crushed Rose" from his playlist and presses play on a chilled number from last year. A few seconds in there's a creaking noise.

Ivy jumps. "Was that the house?"

"It definitely wasn't the music," says Jakob. "I know this track inside out."

"I've been thinking," says Tatum, fidgeting with her phone.

"Uh-oh," says Ivy.

"The predictions." She holds her hand up before we can shout her down. "Hear me out. The 'Something of great value will be lost' — you don't think Steve's binoculars are the thing, do you?"

"I don't care if they're lost for ever," I say.

"That's not the point, Leah," she says. "The point is they're probably worth a lot of money — and they have sentimental value for Steve. Did they turn up before he and your mum went away?"

"No, they didn't. He wants us to keep an eye out for them," I say.

Tatum nods. "I think it's significant the binoculars

are about looking at something more closely." She holds up her phone and I realize she's filming herself. "The third prediction may have come true at Roeshot House. Something of great value will be lost. This could be interpreted in different ways but..." and she rambles on while I look at the other two Amigos and shake my head.

Jakob picks up one of the beanbags and mimes throwing it at Tatum and that cheers me up. He drops it and lands on top of it, pushing himself round the wooden floor to get into shot.

Tatum finishes her report by saying, "The four of us are eagerly waiting to see if Alice Billings's lifelong friend, Margery, is willing to speak to us. A meeting with her might be the next step to unlocking the secrets of what went on all those years ago. Meanwhile we're bracing ourselves in case any further predictions come true."

I roll my eyes at Ivy but her face is serious. Angry. "This isn't a game, Tatum," she says. "I know what you're going to hint at next. You're going to use Poppy's illness for your documentary, aren't you?"

Jakob sits up. "The 'Someone will die'? That's ridiculous."

"Whoa – that's a leap," says Tatum. She holds her hands up with an affronted expression.

"Poppy's going to get better," I say.

Ivy's face frightens me. There are tears in her eyes. "She's getting worse, not better."

I move across the room to her armchair and gently

budge in beside her. "They'll find out what's wrong with her. 'Course they will. You musn't worry about it."

"What do the doctors say?" Jakob asks.

Ivy twists the fringe of the blanket round her fingers. She shrugs. "She's losing weight. She feels sick most of the time. Her hair is falling out. She has no energy. It's really hard to keep her positive. And now Baz..."

My stomach churns at the memory of Baz's broken body by the bins.

"They're doing tests?" I ask.

Ivy nods. "Poppy hates them. She's got a phobia about hospitals now."

Tatum says, "That doesn't surprise me."

I glare at her.

Jakob gets off the beanbag and on to the sofa. "It's partly psychological, though, isn't it?" He says it in an embarrassed way.

Ivy sighs.

"Could it be linked to your dad...?" he asks.

Remember the pact, I want to scream.

Tears roll down Ivy's cheek. She wipes them on the blanket. "Sorry. It's just taking so long for her to be better. I don't know. Maybe it is something to do with Dad, but if it is she's not saying."

"Have the tests shown up anything?" says Jakob. He should stop interrogating her.

She shakes her head.

"So has she seen a psychiatrist or someone like that?"

133

She nods. "We can't make her talk if she doesn't want to."

"Who put Poppy on that diet?" Jakob asks. "Does she mind it?"

"Mum and I researched the best foods for her," Ivy says. "She doesn't eat much, so what she does eat has to be good for her. She often complains her stomach hurts."

"You need answers," says Jakob. "A proper diagnosis."

"We're doing our best," says Ivy. "She's had quite a few treatments already. She's seen loads of different people."

"You need someone to help you eliminate different things," says Jakob. "Someone properly organized. How about Mum? You know what she's like. She won't rest until she's got to the bottom of something. You've only got to ask."

"Thanks, Jakob," says Ivy.

Jakob adds quickly, "On the other hand, you might not want to get Mum involved. She might do your head in and raise the stress levels sky-high. But you need more help." He taps his lip, thinking. "There's this boy at school. His dad is some hotshot doctor, a psychiatrist for kids. He came in to talk to our year group about exam stress. He has people who come from all over the world to see him... I could find out more. You can't let this situation go on and drag you down."

"You're right," says Ivy.

"Let's talk to my mum tonight!"

"No, not tonight, it's New Year's Eve, and I don't want to make Mum sad. Tomorrow."

Tatum blows out her breath really noisily. "Perhaps Poppy's one of those people who find it a struggle to cope in the real world, and there's no cure for that, is there?"

"Er, we're trying to come up with *helpful* solutions here," I say.

"You didn't let me finish," says Tatum. "The fact Poppy reckons she's seen a ghost says something. I reckon it says she's after attention, and you shouldn't fuss around her so much."

"She thinks the ghost was real," says Ivy. She's talking slowly, upset with Tatum. "She really believes she saw it. And I'm not fussing. I'm caring for her."

"OK, then. I've got a good idea," says Tatum. "I'll interview Poppy about the ghost for the documentary. It'll add some atmosphere and if nothing else you might understand more of what's going on in her head." She sees Ivy's horrified expression. "Don't worry. You can sit in on the interview and we can edit out any stuff that makes her sound too whacko." She picks up her phone and pans round the room. She's clearly filming us so I put my hand in front of my face to make a point.

"By the way," she says. "Anyone making any predictions or resolutions tonight?"

"No," the three of us reply at the same time.

SEVENTEEN

Tatum goes off to see if Poppy is up for an interview, but comes straight back saying she's asleep on a sofa.

"I'm surprised you didn't wake her up," says Jakob.

"I wanted to, but Gabs said not to," says Tatum. She flops face-down on to the sofa and says, "Save me from this boredom." A second later she lifts her head and says, "Please tell me you have a secret stash of alcohol."

"Not really," says Ivy. "There's alcohol in the larder. . ."

"But we can't drink now," says Jakob.

"Why not?" asks Tatum.

I roll my eyes. Tatum doesn't seem to understand the most basic of rules. "We've got to go downstairs and eat with the adults soon. They won't trust us go to the

Holiday Village if they think we've been pre-drinking up here. We have to pick our moments strategically."

"My parents would be cool about it," says Tatum.

"Our parents aren't," says Jakob. He glances at me. "How about we play twenty-one dares?"

Ivy groans. "I never get it right," she says. "Twenty-one always lands on me." But I know she'll play. She always does.

We push the sofas nearer the armchair so we're closer together. There's the usual argument about who's going to start.

"We can only say one, two or three numbers?" checks Tatum.

"Yep. One, two," I say, starting. "We're going round clockwise."

"Three, four, five," says Jakob.

"Six," says Ivy.

"Seven, eight, nine," says Tatum. She stretches one arm, then another, as if she's ever so slightly disinterested.

We go round again twice. Twenty-one lands on me.

"Arggh," I say.

"Truth or dare?" sings Ivy.

"Truth." I usually go for truth. "No, wait. Dare."

"Too late," says Ivy.

"Have you ever kissed anyone properly?" asks Tatum. Her expression tells me she's anticipated the answer and thinks it's hilarious.

The other two smile encouragingly at me. They

wonder if anything exciting has happened throughout the year that I haven't told them about.

"No," I say. It feels shameful in front of Tatum.

"Boring question," says Jakob.

"You think so?" says Tatum.

Ivy says, "Next time we have to agree on the question together."

"Next round," says Tatum. "One."

I don't know how it happens because Ivy and I try to work it, without actually verbalizing it, that twenty-one lands on Tatum, but it's Jakob who gets it. He shrieks, "Nooooo," then, "All right, give me a dare. And it can't be 'eat a dead fly' because I had to do that last time we played."

"Go and sneak some alcohol from the larder," says Tatum.

"It's got to be a group decision," I say.

Ivy tightens her tartan blanket round herself and says. "I've got a good one. Jakob has to run round the outside of the house—"

"That's not a dare," says Tatum scornfully.

"With a bare chest," finishes Ivy. "It's below freezing out there."

"I'd like to see him run faster than he's ever run before," I say. "So it's a yes from me."

"And I'd like to film it, so all right," says Tatum.

"Dare accepted, but I'm not taking anything off until the very last minute," says Jakob.

"You have to run the whole way," says Tatum. "If you walk, you have to do another lap."

"How are we going to check he runs all the way?" asks Ivy.

I pat him on the arm. "Don't worry, Jakob. I'll run with you to supervize. But I'm wearing as many layers as I like."

Jakob pats me back and says, "How kind."

"Poppy's definitely going to want to see this if she's awake," says Ivy. "I'll tell her to look out of the conservatory. Wave at her when you go by?"

"Anything else you'd like me to do?" asks Jakob.

"Yes – do an Irish dance by the grave," says Tatum. "Only joking!"

Ivy goes to see if Poppy's awake. Tatum fetches her turquoise coat. I pile on another sweater and a scarf because my coat is in the kitchen and if an adult sees me with it, they'll ask where I'm going and I can't be bothered with that. Jakob goes in search of his beanie hat, saying there was nothing about keeping his head uncovered and it's too late to make any more rules.

We meet by the front door. Ivy says Poppy's woken up and is making her way to the conservatory. Jakob runs on the spot and asks for a countdown for his T-shirt and jumper removal. On zero, he whips them off over his head, squealing. He rushes to replace his hat, and scampers outside, shouting that his nipples will never be the same again.

"No screaming by the kitchen or lounge," I warn him, "or we'll get the why-can't-you-be-sensible lecture."

He nods vigorously. "I ... can't ... speak ... too ... cold."

I laugh and the wind burns the back of my throat.

"Wave at the camera!" instructs Tatum.

I'm not sure how a topless Jakob will fit into the documentary.

Jakob runs surprisingly fast. We pace past the kitchen window, down the side passage, and duck down past the big lounge window. Jakob remembers to wave at Poppy as we sprint past the conservatory. Tatum films us out of the dining-room window, a room so cold and far from the kitchen we rarely use it, and then we follow the path round down the side of the house towards where the rose garden would have been.

The wind's got up now, and as my hair flies across my face, there's a huge body-jolting crash. I instinctively cower. Jakob shouts and I can't work out what he's saying, but he's stopped running, and he's pointing at the ground. At a lump of metal on the path.

"That could have killed us," says Jakob. He wraps his arms round his pale, skinny torso. His face is almost blue.

I hug him and look round, and up. "It's the metal bar from the attic window." I feel wobbly with the shock of it. The near miss.

"Come on," I say, rubbing his back, his delicate, freezing ribs. "Back round to the front door." We run, faster than before, the breath squeezed from our lungs, and when we reach the front door, we scream for the others, and they're there, Tatum, Ivy and then Poppy, asking what the matter is.

I pick up Jakob's T-shirt and jumper and press it against him, but he needs help putting them on because his hands are too shaky.

"The metal bar from the window dropped. It almost hit us," I say. The shock of it catches up with me and I feel tearful. What if we'd been a fraction of a second faster? It was that close.

Tatum rushes off to look at it.

"Jakob needs a hot drink," I say. I lead him into the kitchen like someone who's been rescued from a river and needs warming up, and Elaine, who's there with Auntie Gabs is on her feet, asking what's wrong. I tell her we were having a running race and the metal bar fell. I make some tea while Elaine calls Marc, and the three adults press for more details.

Tatum comes running in with the bar. It's very heavy and the close-up smell of rust is unpleasant. Marc says we'd be within our rights to sue Pinhurst Properties. He goes up to the attic to see how it could have fallen.

I'm worried for Clive and Evan, so I say it gave us a scare but we're OK. Jakob sips his tea and nods. Auntie Gabs asks if she wants me to drive her somewhere to get a signal on my phone to call Mum. I shake my head. There's no point.

Marc comes back downstairs, saying he'll get on to Clive about it right away. "Very shoddy of him not to have maintained the attic window properly," he says as he goes to make the call on his mobile at the end of the drive. Elaine tut-tuts about slipping standards and Clive taking on more projects than he can cope with.

We leave Elaine and Auntie Gabs in the kitchen and go into the lounge, to huddle up on sofas near the fire.

Poppy clings to me, and I like having her close. Jakob sits the other side of me, still quiet from shock. "We'll go out tonight and have a good time," I tell him.

"And celebrate the fact we're still alive," he mutters.

"You're not going to want to hear this," says Tatum. "But Rose's ghost was responsible. She wants revenge."

EIGHTEEN

I spend a while getting my mascara right in the bathroom mirror and thinking about how much I'm looking forward to seeing Evan again and how much I want to dance. There was a tense atmosphere at dinner and I just want to get out of this house. Dancing makes me happy. It clears my head. I'm jumpy with anticipation. I knock on Ivy's door when I'm done because I don't want to be around Tatum more than I have to.

She's curled up on her bed, not even half-ready to go out. "Hi," she says in a quiet voice. "Hope you're all right after that metal bar falling."

I nod. "I want to go out and forget about it. I'll be OK once I've done some dancing."

"That's good," Ivy says. She looks stressed, as if she's been crying. I sit on the end of her bed. "I'm sorry if we upset you by asking so many questions about Poppy."

"You didn't. I was thinking about Baz."

"Don't think about it," I say. "And don't worry about Steve — if there's any evidence, I'm going to the police. I'm not joking. I know they'd say it was an accident or that it happened on private land, but he needs the biggest warning they can give him."

"I'm not sure if I want to come out tonight," she says. "I'm not feeling it."

"You have to," I say. "The Three Amigos stick together through thick or thin. And I need you to stop Tatum flirting with Evan so I have a chance."

She smiles. "Seriously? OK, then."

The adults have made an effort for the evening. Gabs is wearing a garment that has huge sleeves and isn't very practical around the kitchen, Marc has put on his one and only party shirt (or at least the one he's brought to Roeshot House three years in a row) and Elaine has swapped her blue jeans for black ones and has ditched her fleece for a fluffy cardigan.

The bunting goes up every year, strung across the kitchen cupboards, and this year there's a silver theme going on with silver party poppers, candles and napkins. Poppy has styled red-rose decorations out of paper and sellotaped them on to the insides of the kitchen and back doors, which the adults admire but otherwise don't comment on.

Ivy touches one of them and mutters, "Are you getting fixated?"

Poppy says, "What does that mean?"

"She means, did you make those decorations because you're thinking about Rose Strathmortimer?" says Tatum.

"I did it to keep the ghost away," says Poppy. The matter-of-fact way she says it is unsettling.

We Amigos exchange looks, and Tatum raises her eyebrows.

"Okaaaay," says Marc. "Let's stop the conversation there."

We eat a roast meal. I watch Poppy spend a lot of time cutting her food up and only taking a few bites. After a few minutes, she takes a black biro from next to a bowl where she probably left it earlier and draws a panda on her wrist.

Elaine says it feels odd for there to be three adults and five children around the table this year.

"Feeling outnumbered, Mum?" asks Jakob.

We don't notice that Gabs is crying until she gets up, wiping her eyes and smudging her eye make-up.

"Oh, dear," says Elaine, looking at Marc with alarm. "That must have been my fault. Reminding her..." She takes a big sip of wine and says under her breath, "Though I really do think Kate could have been more thoughtful with her plans. New Year's Eve works so much better with more of a crowd." In a brighter voice, she says, "We've had good memories in this house. We've been very lucky. Shall I fetch the dessert?"

We play Monopoly with Poppy until it's time for her to go to bed, then we dash upstairs to check our faces and outfits. We know we're not going to be able to get away with merely sliding out of the back door. Gabs hugs us tightly and I wonder if she's had too much to drink. Elaine and Marc wheel out a lecture: stay safe on the road, take an extra torch, wrap up against the cold and be sensible. When Elaine says, "Now, what I mean by sensible is. . ." Jakob says, "We get it, Mum. We're going now."

We're not used to being outside at night here. The garden with its tall trees feels watchful. We steer clear of the bins where Baz was found, and none of us mentions the grave. We adjust our gloves and scarves, the frosty air stinging our cheeks.

The cows are big, bulky, staring statues as we walk past the field. We're on the other side of the road because it's the only side with pavement, and even that will peter out before we've left Pinhurst. Tatum stops by one of the few streetlights to look at the muddy track that leads to the woods behind the field and Roeshot House. "The entrance to the woods isn't overlooked. Very tempting place to bury a body."

"For God's sake," says Jakob. "Give it a rest."

Tatum has her gloves off and she's holding her

phone at waist height so it tilts up at her face. Is she trying out a new technique? She swings round to film the other side of the road. There's a house there but it's back to front, with the front door out of sight and no windows set in the brick wall that butts up against the pavement. "The woods extend to the back of Roeshot House, again not overlooked. Why did Alice choose the garden? Because it was convenient? Because she wanted to stay close to her sister? Or because she *panicked*?"

I jump at the word panicked. A cat stalks out of the track. It has something moving in its mouth.

We make *eww* sounds and Tatum has her fingers on the screen, zooming in. "Lovely," she says with satisfaction. "Great image."

"They should have more lampposts," I say as we leave the village and bunch together on the road, flattening out against the hedgerow when we hear cars coming, our feet sinking into the soft, muddy verges. It's hard not to think about Baz being hit by a car.

"I have a super-glarey reflective tabard from when I took a cycling safety class in Year Five," says Ivy. "I so wish I was wearing it now."

"My shoes are in a right state. I should have worn my hiking boots and brought these in a bag," says Jakob.

I say I wish I knew the names of the stars. I remind the others of the dance-offs we used to have in the attic, the routines I used to make up and teach them.

Tatum is the only one who doesn't need to distract herself from the creepy silence.

As soon as we see the huge lit-up entrance sign for the Holiday Village, we speed up.

"Oh, look – a signpost to the spa," says Tatum. "This place is civilized. Why wouldn't you stay here instead of Roe*shit* House?"

We go past rows of neat mobile homes, and hear the occasional burst of laughter or murmur of conversation through a window. Old-fashioned lanterns attached to posts light the way.

The most exciting sight is the free Wi-Fi sign on the window of the reception. Before we do anything else we go in and ask the girl on duty for the password. She asks us which mobile home we're from and straight-off Tatum says, "Thirty-seven."

The girl frowns but tells us the password.

We hover near the door for quite a while, checking our phones. Sofia's sent me a selfie of her and Dan with his nan. Their relationship has developed so quickly that she's spending New Year's Eve with his family? I send a photo back of me next to a poster advertising the disco.

I write Dad an early Happy New Year text so I don't need to think about it later. I reply to Mum's text, saying everything is fine. I purposely don't ask how her two-day break is going, and I don't mention the Steve theory in case he scrubs away any blood or fixes any dents on the car.

"I can see Evan," says Tatum, and I follow where she's

looking, and see him too. He's with a group of maybe fifteen people, sitting around a couple of tables in the bar area. Dance music thuds away from a room at the back. There are a lot of family groups, and two little girls skip about in sparkly outfits trying to drag their dad off to the disco.

Evan stands up when he sees us, surprised but also pleased. "You made it!" To the others, he says, "These are the guys I told you about, the ones staying in Roeshot House," which makes me curious about what exactly he's told them. He rattles off his friends' names, and the only ones I can remember afterwards are Kai and Megan, who seem to be a couple. Kai tells us to give him money for drinks if we want alcohol because his brother is behind the bar. Tatum hands over some notes and says we can pay her back later, and we give our orders.

"You're lucky we made it," says Jakob. "The big metal bar across the attic window fell down inches from my head this afternoon. Leah and me were almost killed!"

Evan swears so loudly the group next to us turn and stare. "How? That's terrible. Does my dad know?"

I nod and tell him what happened, and Evan rubs his face and says how sorry he is and how he can't believe our bad luck.

"Or good luck, perhaps," I say. "It missed us."

His friends ask us what it's like to stay in Roeshot House knowing about Rose's body, and Tatum, who never even knew what it was like before, answers for us, saying there's already been another death: Baz's. She describes in horrible detail how she was the one to find him, and how when she vomited, it bounced off the leaves of the plants. "I reckon the car must have been going super-fast to mash Baz up like that," she says, shuddering away the thought. She moves on to Poppy's ghost and the falling metal bar and we hiss at her to stop. "Something's been unleashed and we've all got to watch our backs," she says.

"The house feels weird," I concede. "But maybe that's because we know about the body."

"It's also because Ivy's little sister's not well," says Jakob. "She's got a mystery illness."

At first I think Ivy is going to sink into her chair in embarrassment but then she tells the others about the treatments Poppy's had, and the many hospital appointments, some of which Ivy has to take her to.

"So you're like a carer?" says Megan.

"Sort of. It's just me and my mum and sometimes she has ... down days."

"You know that friend I was telling you about, whose dad is a child psychiatrist?" says Jakob. "I messaged him just now and he says his dad will help. So Poppy could come to stay with us for a while and get to see him, while you and your mum have a break."

Ivy widens her eyes. "You mean it?"

"Of course."

"Did he definitely say yes?"

"Don't worry about it. I'll make it happen," says Jakob. "I promise."

I give him a thumbs-up that no one else can see. The mood shifts. We leave death and illness behind, sipping our drinks and listening to the music escaping from the disco. There's a discussion about the new menu at the Chinese takeaway, the locals agreeing that the old menu should never have been tampered with, and that the introduction of kebabs is a mistake, followed by an argument over who changed someone's default language to Bulgarian on their phone.

Evan remembers the burning thing he temporarily forgot to tell us because he was distracted by the news of the window bar. Donna texted him to say Margery has invited us round tomorrow morning to discuss the memorial. "Meet outside the takeaway at ten to ten. She's expecting us at ten and we can't be late."

"Is that Margery who taught us the violin?" asks Kai. "That woman used to give me nightmares."

"Yup," says Evan. "This lot want to find out more about Alice Billings – so Mum's friend Donna suggested we speak to her. Tatum's doing a video project. I said I'd help. All part of the concierge service. Keeping the customers happy." He bows with mock-obsequiousness.

"I couldn't stay in that house," says Megan. "I'd have gone home by now."

Tatum opens her mouth. I'm pretty sure she's about to say something rude, but she remembers Evan is there and she needs his cooperation if she's ever going to get to meet Margery.

"We're still mostly having a good time," I say because I want it to be true.

Jakob raises an eyebrow. It means: *Baz's death, the metal bar incident, Poppy's strange illness and Tatum taking over.* But it also means *Amigos together again, we're out for the first time ever on New Year's Eve, and am I right in thinking you totally fancy Evan?*

"Next time you come, it'll be cool again," says Evan. "The police will work out the full story and the ghosts will settle down."

Kai comes back with the drinks and conversation breaks out in smaller groups.

"The police might never work out the full story," I say to Evan.

"True," he says. "But maybe soon we'll know how Rose died. That's what most people want to know, isn't it?" He shrugs. "So. Let's dance."

"Sure," I say because I'd never do that thing of being too shy to dance, or waiting to be persuaded.

Evan says, "Who's coming?"

Across the table, Ivy gives me a quick smile and a raise of her shoulders to show she's excited for me.

A few of Evan's friends, including Kai and Megan, stand up, and so does Jakob. Ivy shakes her head and picks up her rum and coke. Tatum says she needs to Facetime her friends, and interview some of Evan's group.

"You sure, Ivy?" I ask. I can't tell if she's just trying to give me space.

"Feeling tired," she says. She holds up her drink and says she'll come and find us when she's finished it. I feel a pang of guilt for forcing her out tonight.

The disco floor is populated with four couples and the little girls who are holding hands with their dad. Jakob goes to the other end of the room and does two backflips in quick succession.

"Oi!" barks the old-man DJ through his microphone. "You're going to hurt someone. Cut it out."

Jakob grins and starts dancing, exaggerated and energetic, then slinky and over-the-top sexy. It makes me laugh. This is so what I need.

I spin and swirl and take up too much space. I relax, knowing that the happy version of myself is emerging. I sing the lyrics with Jakob, and mirror his movements.

It seems inevitable that sooner or later I'll dance with Evan. He holds his hands out to me and I hesitate for one beat. Is it really me he wants to dance with?

His face and body come more into focus as everything else blurs. I see the brightness of his eyes and the pleasing lines of his body.

"Hi," he says.

"Hi," I reply.

"Ready?" he says, and in response to whatever he's asking, I nod and trust. Beat after glorious beat pumps through me. Pink lights. Orange, yellow, red. Bright white squares of light rotating. My muscles are warm and fluid. All my senses are pulsing and at their peak, and this is how I imagine it is to be high.

The song ends and I pull away, but he catches the ends of my fingers. "Stay." He leans in and takes a strand of hair that's fallen across my face and tucks it behind my ear. I want him to do it again. To touch my skin in that gentle way. He smiles as he takes my hands again, and I squeeze them ever so slightly, testing the connection. He squeezes back.

We dance on and on. I mouth the lyrics when I wasn't aware I knew them, and everything is how it should be, the music, Evan, me.

"Leah?" Tatum has her hand near her mouth. She's going to cup it against my ear so I can hear what she's saying. At first her breath tickles and I giggle.

"Ivy's not feeling well. We should leave," she says, and I pull back. "She's got a migraine." The words hiss down my ear.

"What's the matter?" asks Evan.

"We need to go back," says Tatum, almost shouting so he can hear her. "Ivy's ill."

He registers concern and I wave across at Jakob to join us, and we walk into the bar.

"Ivy's in reception," says Tatum when she sees me looking for her. "It's not as noisy there."

She's lying on a sofa, clutching her head in her hands. It must be bad if she doesn't care about lying down in reception.

"Ivy, are you OK?" asks Jakob, reaching her before me.

She says. "I've got a splitting headache. I think it was a combination of the alcohol and the lighting."

"We'll take you home," I say.

She turns her head very slowly. "Wait until after midnight. Honestly. I'm not going to ruin your night."

I remember holding Evan's hand. The dizzying possibility of him leaning in for a kiss. "It's OK," I say, and then whisper, "Amigos first."

"I'll walk back with you," says Evan.

"Very gallant," says Tatum with a touch of sarcasm. "But we'll get a taxi. I've got cash." She goes to the reception desk where the girl looks thrilled to have something to do.

I step away from the other two, and say to Evan, "Thanks for inviting us. See you outside the takeaway tomorrow."

"Wish you didn't have to leave early," he says.

"Me too," I say and then Tatum calls Evan over to the reception desk. The taxi driver is coming from Riddingham and needs the postcode of Roeshot House.

It's not far off midnight when we finally get into the taxi.

"I can't believe I'm doing this to you," says Ivy as she sits next to me. "You and Evan were getting on so well."

"He's really nice," I say.

Tatum turns round from the front passenger seat. "All part of his concierge service, like he said. I wouldn't go thinking you're special. And who knows, maybe you're the one who's unlucky in love?"

NINETEEN

Tatum is filming as she steps out of the taxi, having paid the driver. She doesn't go directly to the back door with Ivy, Jakob and me. She veers off to the grave and talks about it being several minutes to midnight, and asks what fresh horror the New Year will bring to the residents of Roeshot House now that the body of Rose Strathmortimer has been disturbed.

"She's the one who's disturbed," says Ivy through clenched teeth.

"She's definitely making the most of your headache," I say. "Getting us back just before midnight."

Jakob says, "She's jealous of you and Evan, that's why."

Tatum has crept up behind us. "You think I'm jealous

of Leah and Evan? Give me some credit. He's been great setting up interviews, but he's very, very average."

"Keep telling yourself that," I snap at her.

Tatum holds her hands up, laughing. "OK, OK! I guess I'll leave that one alone."

The frost has made silvery claws of thin branches, and crouching statues of the overgrown plants. Something suddenly looms over me and I squeal.

"It's just a cow's shadow," laughs Tatum. "Relax!"

As we get nearer to the house, we hear Marc's voice in the darkness. "You're back early. Everything all right?" His footsteps echo down the side passage.

"Ivy's got a bad headache so we came home," says Jakob when Marc appears, pulling his coat round himself, his arms not in the sleeves.

We pile into the warmth of the kitchen and into the lounge where Gabs and Elaine are drinking red wine. They hug us as if we've been away for days, breathing their alcohol fumes over us, making a fuss over Ivy, feeling her forehead, wondering where the paracetamol went. Before we have time to prepare, it's midnight and there are more hugs and "Auld Lang Syne" sung along with the people on the TV. Ivy has too much of a headache to join in, so I'm in between Jakob and Auntie Gabs. Auntie Gabs's hand is dry and bony, and her eyes are shining as if she might be holding back tears.

"Bet Kate's wishing she were here," says Elaine. "You can't beat New Year's Eve at Roeshot House. Still, I

expect she's having a nice time with that chap of hers."
She smiles at me.

I don't smile back.

"My best New Year's Eve was in the Caribbean," says
Tatum.

I see Elaine look at Marc with annoyance.

"Stay here and play charades," says Auntie Gabs.
"Count me out, though. I should be getting to bed. I'm so
damn tired."

"I think we should all turn in, to be honest," says
Elaine.

"Quit while we're ahead," agrees Marc. "Wake up
in good time for a trip to the castle the other side of
Riddingham."

Castle. We all look at each other in alarm.

I look at Jakob and mouth, *Margery.*

"We've got plans for tomorrow," says Jakob. "Meeting
up with a few of Evan's friends."

"Oh, honestly," says Elaine.

"We'll talk about it in the morning," says Marc,
tugging on Elaine's arm. "'Night, all." The three adults
go upstairs, shouting back to us to remember to switch off
the lights.

If Ivy didn't have such a bad headache, and if Tatum
wasn't with us, I know we Amigos would be raiding the
larder for biscuits and sweets to take up to the attic. Or
we'd be planning to congregate in one of our bedrooms.
We'd climb into the same bed and tell each other ghost

stories about heads on sticks banging against windows and sinister dolls. Tonight, none of us are hungry. We wait for Ivy to get a glass of water while Tatum tells us how we're going to have to steer the conversation with Margery so that we get off the subject of a memorial as soon as possible and on to Alice Billings herself.

"If Alice and Margery were school friends, Margery is likely to have met Rose," says Tatum. "That would be wonderful: a first-hand account of Rose. I want to know about Doug Billings as well. He must have known what was going on. Alice wasn't that big, so would she have been able to bury a body on her own? How long would that take, with no one noticing? And why did he die three years after Rose? Was it really a heart attack?"

I glance at Ivy but she's found the paracetamol and is taking a couple of tablets.

"I'll lead the questions," says Tatum. "Evan's not going to want to do it, though he'd be best, given she knows him."

"She's won't like you filming her," says Jakob.

"I'll be subtle." She pauses. "I can be subtle, you know."

We walk through the house together, turning off the lights as we go. We don't say it out loud, but none of us would want to be doing this on our own. At the half-open door of the little lounge, Ivy pauses to see if she can hear whether Poppy is asleep. We hear her turn over in bed, making a whimpering sound which makes me wonder if she is dreaming about Baz.

The hallway is in gloom even with the lights on, and we notice the difference in temperature as we walk through to our side of the house. The smell changes too, from food and an open fire, to slight damp and old fabrics.

Ivy and Tatum are ahead of me and Jakob on the stairs. I strain to hear what Tatum is saying to Ivy. It's something about the Holiday Village. Beside me, Jakob hums one of his violin pieces.

I have a sense of déjà vu as Ivy slips on the stair with the loose carpet. Tatum and Ivy fall into each other and Ivy drops her glass of water. I watch it bounce as they both step back into Jakob. He's screaming and falling and I spin round, too late to catch him, shouting at him to reach for the banister, but the words are clogged in my throat because it's happening too fast and I'm too agonizingly slow. The glass smashes. The noise as Jakob hits another step, unable to save himself, and lands on the hard floor at the bottom is a double thud followed by an inhuman noise of pure pain. He lies on his side, his arm underneath him, a leg at an angle that's wrong.

I reach him first, shaky and nauseous, the other two thundering back down the stairs behind me. His eyes tell me he's only half-conscious, and I scream for Elaine, Marc and Auntie Gabs, for someone to tell us what to do, and how to help him. He's panting, eyes rolling. There are three or four tiny pieces of glass embedded in his face.

"What happened?" Marc appears in a dressing gown.

Elaine is still dressed. Their faces have sagged with shock. "One of you call an ambulance!" Marc screams. "Go to the end of the driveway for a signal. Now!"

Tatum has her phone ready. Of course she does. She runs to the front door and out into the cold night with only a thin wrap-top over her dress

Marc holds Jakob's hand and tells him that he needs to stay still and breathe in and out. Auntie Gabs appears, with crumpled clothing and messed-up hair, as if she's been lying on her bed fully clothed. "I'll drive you to hospital," she says.

"You've drunk too much," says Marc.

"We shouldn't move him," says Elaine. "Tatum's calling an ambulance."

Jakob whimpers and he clutches his dad's hand more tightly. I hear a noise further up the hallway and see a small pale figure. Poppy. Her face is fearful.

"Jakob fell," says Elaine. "He's hurt." She's crying. I've never seen her cry.

"Come here, Pops," says Auntie Gabs. She ushers Poppy back into the little lounge.

Ivy sweeps up the smashed glass and it seems ages before Tatum comes back, her teeth chattering from the cold, red-raw hands pulling her top round her. She says the ambulance is on its way.

"Thanks," says Marc. "Jakob, you're going to be all right. What were you doing? Were you fooling around? How much have you drunk?"

Jakob grimaces. The pink bits in his hair look silly, as if we coloured them in with a permanent marker.

He shakes his head. "Ivy slipped and fell into Tatum. They stepped backwards. . ." he gasps. "My ankle twisted. I'm not drunk."

"It was the loose carpet," says Ivy.

"I'm sorry," says Tatum.

"Me too," says Ivy.

Two paramedics arrive and they assess Jakob and say they're pretty sure he's broken his arm and his leg and his ankle is badly twisted. They say he'll need an operation. As they move him carefully, screaming with pain despite an injection, on to a stretcher, I remember the prediction: *There will be an unexpected twist of fate.*

I wonder if Tatum's phone was recording when he fell.

TWENTY

After Elaine goes off in the ambulance with Jakob, with Marc following by car, Auntie Gabs says, "That was traumatic. My heart breaks for that boy. I'll go back to the little lounge and check Poppy's asleep. Will you three be all right? Sure?"

Ivy, Tatum and I go upstairs carefully. I hold on to the banister tightly. At the top we say goodnight and we hug. I still feel shaky.

"Poor Jakob," says Ivy softly.

"Poor Jakob," echoes Tatum.

I nod.

I think I'll never fall asleep. I expect Tatum to talk endlessly about her theories, but she's silent.

*

The next thing I know, light is edging through the gap in the curtains and there are strange scratching, fluttering noises coming from outside. I freeze. It could be someone trying to break in through the window. I listen harder, distracted by the pounding of my heart. My body is slick with sweat by the time I work it out; it's a bird on the windowsill. I breathe in and out slowly, and think of Jakob in hospital, shocked, grey-faced, pink-haired. I wonder what time his operation is scheduled for, or if they operated as soon as they got him to the hospital.

I fumble for my phone to check the time. I don't want to miss meeting Evan; he's the one good thing that's come out of this holiday. My memories of last night are a mix of horror at Jakob's fall, but also pleasure at dancing with Evan. There was definitely something sparking between us. But perhaps he got carried away because it was New Year's Eve? He might be embarrassed to see me this morning.

I have to get moving if I want a shower and a quick breakfast. I go into the bathroom. It's cold, bare and unwelcoming. The heater ticks loudly when I pull the cord, but the heated bar doesn't go orange. When I've showered, I knock on Ivy's door, and open it.

"Morning," she says in a groggy voice. I've woken her up. She looks fragile, still tired out after a night's sleep.

Tatum is awake when I go back into our room.

She's talking in a low voice into her phone, recording something, and stops when she sees me in the doorway. "Any news about Jakob?" she asks.

"'Course not," I say. "No one's been to the end of the drive yet."

Tatum rolls her eyes. "This place. It's not romantic with no signal or Wi-Fi, or even a basic *payphone*. It's dangerous. Imagine if you didn't have anyone to run to the end of the driveway to call an ambulance." Her eyes meet mine.

"I'm going downstairs," I say, not wanting to think about that.

Poppy is in the kitchen drawing comic strips. She tells me it's about a ghost-girl who isn't really a ghost but everyone thinks she is so they don't take any notice of her and so she's able to go round solving crimes and beating bullies.

I look at her precise pictures and try not to think about Jakob. Or Tatum.

"You've got so good at drawing over the last year," I say.

"That's because I've practised a lot," says Poppy. She pushes up her sleeve. "Drawing and reading."

I point to the Sharpie marks on her arm. "What's the tattoo?"

"Not my best one," says Poppy. "It's a plant growing up my arm. Did I tell you I'm going to be a tattoo fixer? People are going to come to me when they have a scar or a tattoo that's gone wrong and I'll make it into something really cool."

I tug her sleeve up and the inside of her arm is covered in leaves of different greens with a big purple flower at the elbow. "Pretty," I say.

Poppy pulls down her sleeve and says, "Don't make me eat breakfast."

"You have to eat something," I say and ask her what she wants to eat.

When she says chocolate, we sneak into the larder and I make a bargain with her. I'll let her have a slice of Terry's Chocolate Orange if she eats a few mouthfuls of fruit salad. She agrees but it takes her ages to nibble the chocolate, and when I place the fruit in front of her she takes a bite of apple and says it tastes sour.

"Should have made you eat the fruit first," I say, hitting my head with the palm of my hand.

She smiles. "I might eat it later."

"That would be great!" I say, squeezing her arm.

She winces and I apologize for forgetting about her muscle aches. In my head I also apologize for not being willing to stay home and spend time with her when I have Evan and Margery to meet.

I tell her we're going to meet Evan's friends and that Auntie Gabs will be down soon, and she settles down in the lounge to watch a film on her iPad.

We leave a little extra time so we can check our phones on the way. Tatum tells me not to be surprised if Mum has an announcement. I ask her what she's on about.

"You're dense if you don't think them going away, just

the two of them, doesn't mean anything," she says as we walk down the driveway.

"It's not just the two of them," I say. "Steve's sister is there. And her husband and kids."

"Steve's introducing your mum to his family. Don't you think that's significant? Look, I know you don't think so, but I'm just being kind, preparing you for the inevitable."

"Sure, sure," I say, as if I don't believe a word of what she's saying. I resist jogging ahead but the moment I have signal, I scan for a message from Mum. She's sent one saying there's snow where they are and she and Steve are going to delay their return journey until tomorrow, and won't be back until the afternoon. She hopes Gabs and Elaine won't give her too hard a time for that but better to be safe than sorry. It doesn't sound as if she's keeping anything back of significance, but when I tell Tatum that she says, "Wait and see. I hope the snow doesn't wash away any evidence from the car." I message Mum back to let her know about Jakob and to say there's no snow in Pinhurst.

No messages from Jakob. I don't even know if he had his phone on him when he fell. It might still be in his room. No messages from either Elaine or Marc, but I wasn't expecting any. They don't know my number. They'd have contacted Gabs, who we still haven't seen this morning.

Evan is already there outside the takeaway and he opens his arms when he sees us. "Morning!" he shouts, and when we reach him, he says, "Where's Jakob? Overslept?"

He looks distressed when we tell him, especially when we say it was because of the loose carpet. "Could this week get any worse for you?" he says quietly.

"Or you, to be honest," says Tatum. "There are so many things at Roeshot House which need to be fixed."

"Hey," I say. "It's not Evan's fault."

"It's his dad's, then," says Tatum.

Evan looks pained. "Dad's going round this morning to look at the window. I hope Ivy's mum will show him the carpet too. I'm sure we'll compensate you, obviously, but I don't know how that works. Money back or whatever."

"It's not been the best few days," says Ivy.

"But it's been interesting," says Tatum.

"*You're* feeling better, though, yeah?" Evan says to Ivy.

She nods. "Sleeping helped, but I still don't feel a hundred per cent, especially after Jakob's fall."

He takes my hands and squeezes them, and it's all I need to know that it's OK and he's not embarrassed by whatever it was that happened between us last night. He's delighted we've pinched a jar of homemade rhubarb jam from the larder to give to Margery as a gift – if Auntie Gabs notices it's gone, we'll say one of us dropped it and had to throw it away.

"Let's bounce," he says and leads the way. I walk next to him, and the other two drop back. The closed-in feeling I had earlier at Roeshot House disappears as he talks about what happened on his walk back from the Holiday Village in the early hours (loud singing, looking for someone's earring in the dark, Megan and Kai arguing).

"Nice that she wants to be involved with the memorial, don't you think?"

I make a non-committal sound; I missed the switch in conversation.

"Dad's not going to want anything obvious. He probably doesn't want anything at all. He doesn't even know we're seeing her, but I'll have to speak to him soon before Margery bumps into him and says something."

Margery's flat is in a low-rise modern block, within easy walking distance of Silverways. Tatum asks us to film her standing outside. On camera she says being granted access to Alice Billings's friend of over seven decades is the most exciting development in the investigation so far. Off camera she says Margery is going to be a tough nut to crack.

"Imagine being friends for someone that long," I say.

"And then they turn out to have kept a massive secret from you," says Ivy.

"OK, listen up," says Tatum. "I'm going to ask Margery if she minds me filming her. I'm telling her the documentary is a school project and it's going to be about memorials in general, not specifically Rose. I think she'll like that."

Evan gives her a dubious look. "I don't think she will."

"Where's your optimism?" says Tatum. "Right, let's do this!" She films herself pressing the buzzer on the communal door.

The first thing that strikes me when I see Margery is how blue her eyes are. They match her fitted, long-sleeved dress. She's not the stretchy, comfortable trouser type. Her grey hair is in an immaculate bob, and she has the longest neck ever, or maybe it only seems that way because she stands so straight. She reminds me of my dance teacher.

We cram into her hall, and introduce ourselves.

"Do any of you play the violin, like Evan here?" I think about Jakob, as we three girls shake our heads.

When Ivy hands over the jam, Margery says rhubarb is her favourite.

She's not very scary until Tatum asks whether she can film our discussions, and then she cuts Tatum off mid-flow and says, "Certainly not." Tatum says in that case please could she have a photo, and after a disapproving "hmmm", Margery agrees, not realizing that Tatum is filming instead of taking a still, and she doesn't turn her phone off as we walk into the lounge.

The overheated room is rammed with photos of children with perfect hair, and students in graduation outfits who she tells us are her nieces and nephews. There's a piano and several violin cases, and piles of sheet music. The room has doors that lead out on to a very small patio and communal gardens where a dad is playing football with a little boy.

We sit on velvety sofas, and watch Evan bring in cups and saucers on a tray, and then a teapot and milk jug.

"Do any of you take sugar?" asks Margery. "No? How sensible." She asks Evan to fetch a dining-room chair for her to sit on.

We talk about the weather, then Margery asks us how many times we've stayed in Roeshot House. Ivy says she can't remember a New Year that wasn't spent there. I nod in agreement and Tatum says nothing.

Margery asks us what we think of the house and I say, "It's amazing." I notice Tatum raise her eyebrow, and hope Evan didn't see it.

"Alice's favourite part of the house was the garden," says Margery. "The rose garden she planted was incredible. It used to be open to the public once a year." She looks into her teacup. "Of course now I understand the significance of the roses."

We nod and lean forward, holding our cups and saucers still. Our breathing is synchronized. In, out, in out. Waiting.

"I gather from Donna you're keen to establish some kind of memorial to Rose and would like my input."

We nod enthusiastically, and Tatum asks Margery what she'd recommend.

"Well," says Margery. She places her cup and saucer on a little table and clasps her hands together. "I've been thinking about this. Resurrecting the rose garden would be an obvious thing to do, but that was Alice's memorial. I think you should consider something completely new."

"Did you ever meet Rose?" asks Tatum.

Margery says, "Yes. I knew her a bit. I was at school with Alice and I visited her parents' home once or twice, so I met little Rose then. I also saw her a few times when she was staying at Roeshot House. Rose was a lively girl. Not one for sitting still. She loved being outdoors and wildlife. She wasn't very conventional. I remember her telling me once how she was never going to get married like her sister. Most of us were quite keen to get married in those days. It was the done thing. I married in my thirties, which was considered very late."

"How did Rose and Alice get on?" I ask.

Margery sighs. "She was extremely fond of her sister," she says. "That's one of the reasons I find all this so difficult to understand. Alice's father died when Rose was little, and their mother could be very domineering. Alice was protective of Rose, a very responsible sort of person. She sometimes found her sister a little high-spirited, but I thought they got on very well. One of Rose's favourite things was to play croquet. She used to beg everyone who visited to play and I can picture her now, having a game with Alice and Doug and whoever else might be around."

"Do you think Rose took her own life?" asks Tatum.

Margery frowns. "I wouldn't like to speculate," she says.

There's a pause. Did Tatum go too far?

"What was Doug like?" asks Tatum. "Was he fun, or serious?"

Margery leans back on her chair. "Oh, he was very serious." That's all she appears to want to say about Doug.

I can see Tatum dying to ask more, but Margery says, "So, tell me, what ideas have you had about the memorial?"

We shift uncomfortably. "That's why we wanted to ask you," says Evan. "We hadn't got further than something like a bench."

"Oh, that wouldn't do at all," says Margery. "No, I think you need something fun for Rose."

"Like a croquet set," says Ivy.

Margery's eyes widen. "What a splendid idea. I would be quite willing to fund a croquet set for Roeshot House if your father got the lawn in good order, Evan. A croquet lawn should be well maintained and cut to the required length. I can look up the rules."

We look at each other. "I'll speak to Dad," says Evan, and I love that he's willing to risk angering his dad because we wanted to find out more about Alice and Rose. "I'd like to make a bird box too," he adds, and I realize he feels a connection to Rose, and I like that too.

"That's a lovely idea," says Margery. She's smiling and animated – and that must be why Tatum risks the next question:

"Did you ever suspect Alice was hiding something from you? It was a big secret for her to have kept."

Margery says, "If you want to put your cup down,

please would you put it on that coaster, not directly on the table."

"Sorry," says Tatum.

"I never thought Alice was hiding anything of that magnitude, but she did have a breakdown of sorts about a year after John was born. I thought it was because Rose had run away after an unhappy love affair in Switzerland. That's what we were all told. Doug died when John was very young but, in many ways that made life easier for Alice."

"What d'you mean?" I ask.

She looks embarrassed. "I've no wish to gossip."

"Didn't she get on with Doug?" asks Tatum.

"He was a demanding man," says Margery. "I always felt Alice rushed into marriage with him to escape her mother." She slaps her hands down on her lap with finality and says, "I've forgotten to bring through the digestive biscuits."

She disappears into the kitchen and Tatum pans her phone camera round the room, until Evan puts his hand in front of it, and the three of us growl at her to put it away. I look out of the patio doors, at the dad and the boy playing football. The sight stabs me with sadness. I think about the times Dad used to take me to my dance classes. How occasionally when he thought he or I needed cheering up, or there was something to celebrate, we'd take the extra-long route so we could go to the drive-through McDonald's for a McFlurry.

I look at Ivy next to me, who's repositioning a velvety cushion behind her back. I shouldn't let myself feel so sad about Dad when the truth is I can still see him, if I make the effort.

"Was that your phone?" Ivy asks, nodding towards my pocket.

It's a text message from Mum, who's been in touch with Elaine. I relay the message: "Jakob's had an operation to pin his leg, but he needs another one on his arm tomorrow."

"Ouch," says Evan.

"He won't be able to take his violin exam now," I say.

"Result!" says Tatum, laughing.

I shake my head, feeling my face flush with anger. "You don't understand. Yes, he moaned about his violin practice but he always did it. He secretly loved it. You heard him through his bedroom door. He was really good. He'll be gutted."

Margery comes back with a plate of biscuits and says, "What's this?" in a sharp voice, and I tell her about Jakob falling down the stairs.

"He played the violin," adds Tatum, unhelpfully.

"How dreadful. I'd have loved to have heard him play." She commands us to take a digestive and not drop crumbs on the carpet. "Such a pity you didn't continue with lessons, Evan."

Evan squirms. "I wasn't any good. I remember you playing a piece to us with loads of twiddly bits, though, that started off slow and then became faster and faster. We all loved that."

"Really?" says Margery. "You remember that? Well, I never. I still play that piece to keep my fingers moving."

"Can I hear it again?" asks Evan.

Margery hesitates, but not for long. "I'd be delighted," she says.

From a shiny case, Margery picks up the bow and tightens, then lifts a golden-coloured violin and tunes it, the noise far from tuneful. There's a moment's silence before Margery moves her upper body decisively, and starts with a long mournful note. The pace picks up little by little and before long the twiddly notes that Evan mentioned come in, and Margery's fingers move faster and faster.

I look around the room, and imagine I can feel Alice's presence here, late in her life, visiting a friend but burdened with regret. I wish I could feel Rose's lively presence and understand her more. Of course, she'd never have been here. This flat wouldn't have been built in the fifties. The violin piece twists and twirls, becoming ever more frantic, and I look out of the patio doors. The dad and the boy have disappeared, but something else catches my eye. To the left hand side of the doors, I see the stone dragon statue from the photo in the book of gardens that we found in the attic.

TWENTY-ONE

"The dragon," I say, when Margery has played the final chord with a flourish, and we've applauded loudly. "Please, could I have a look at it?"

"What?" mouths Tatum, but as she goes over to see what I'm looking at she recognizes it too. "That was in the photo of Rose, outside the conservatory!"

"Alice gave it to me when she went to live at Silverways. I'd always admired it," says Margery. She seems more comfortable with us now she's played her violin.

The dragon has a chipped wing but he's still fierce-looking. "Alice's grandfather bought it for her in China," says Margery, patting the dragon's rough stone head. "It was supposed to bring luck. Doug thought it was ugly, so it wasn't allowed at the front of the house."

"I think he's gorgeous," I say, and bend down to look the dragon in the eye. How much luck did he bring Alice? "How could Doug not like him?"

Margery says, "The house was his before he and Alice married, and he had it how he wanted, I suppose. The garden was Alice's domain, though. It was very overgrown when she married him, and she transformed it. Come back inside and wipe your feet on the mat. I have some old photos of the garden, if you'd like to see them."

"Yes, please," says Tatum. As Margery goes into the flat first, Tatum whispers, "Let me handle this."

There's a piece of wooden furniture in the corner of the room. Margery pulls out two wooden struts at each side, and brings down the sloped lid to rest on them to make a desk. She opens a small drawer at the back of the desk and lifts out a small pile of photos. "I've taken these out of some old photo albums I had, and I'm going to send them to Alice's son, John. I think he'd like them." She sifts through them and finds the dullest black-and-white photo of a garden I've ever seen, far worse than the one of daffodils in the book in the attic.

We agree with Margery that the garden was indeed lovely. There are a couple more shots of the garden but quite a few photos still in Margery's hand.

"We'd love to see any more photos," says Tatum. At least her phone is safely in her pocket.

Margery fans out the photos like a pack of cards and

says, "I don't suppose there's any harm." She selects one from the pack. "This was Alice before she met Doug, when she was at secretarial college." We gaze at a young, smiling woman with dark hair pulled up from her forehead so it sticks up slightly before rolling back.

"She looks happy," I say and Tatum shakes her head at me as if I've said something lame.

"Ah, she had long hair then," says Tatum. She turns to us to check we've caught the link to Poppy's ghost.

"That was a really happy stage of her life," says Margery, more to herself than us. She hands round the other photos. There's one of Alice with a cross-looking toddler in her arms. "John was actually a sweet boy," says Margery. "When Alice asked me to be his legal guardian if anything ever happened to her and Doug, I was touched. I don't see much of him now he lives in America, but I'm very fond of him. And proud; he's a talented musician."

Margery stares at the next photo for a couple of seconds, then says, "This is Alice and Doug on their wedding day on the lawn at Roeshot House. They had their reception there."

I look over Ivy's shoulder as she holds the photo. Alice looks young and smiley. Doug is a fair bit older and good-looking. They make a handsome couple.

"What did Doug die from?" asks Tatum.

"A heart attack, nothing suspicious," says Margery sharply.

I look at Ivy, to check she's OK at the mention of a heart attack. She clenches her eyes shut for a brief moment.

I place my arm round her shoulder and give her a gentle sideways hug.

"*This*," continues Margery, "is Rose, with Alice and their mother on the lawn at Roeshot House."

We crowd round to glimpse Rose. She's a bridesmaid, wearing the sort of dress I'm planning for my school prom, tightly fitted then flared at the waist. Her dark hair is loose with white flowers attached on one side. She's laughing and the resemblance between the sisters is obvious but Rose is more carefree and, in this picture at least, beautiful. Alice is smiling more formally, posing for the camera, unaware Rose is standing side-on, holding her bouquet like a rounders or baseball bat. Their mother stands upright in a stiff-looking heavy coat and a puffy hat, a handbag in the crook of her elbow. There's no mistaking the smugness in her expression.

Margery gazes at the photo. "Alice was a decent person and a loyal friend. I just can't reconcile her with the person who withheld information about her sister's death and led me to believe Rose was living in Switzerland. She must have had her reasons." She gathers up the photos and says, "I'm feeling a bit tired now. Let me know, Evan, what you decide to do in memory of Rose."

After we've left the flat, Tatum wants to sneak round into the communal gardens to film the dragon statue.

"I can't believe you filmed in her house when she told you you didn't want you to," I say.

"Calm down," she says. "This documentary's for my showreel. Margery will never see it."

"It'll be embarrassing for Evan if Margery sees you out of her patio windows," says Ivy.

Tatum compromises by filming the dragon from a point where we're certain Margery won't be able to see her, then Evan agrees to film Tatum walking from the entrance to the flats to the pavement, as she describes the photos which she wasn't able to film. He has to do three takes because the first time she goes out of focus and the second time she stumbles over a stone. She has to check her nose isn't too red from the cold before she's satisfied with what he's recorded.

"It's snowing where Mum and Steve are," I say. "They can't get back until tomorrow afternoon."

"Snow here would be a challenge for my lighting, but it would add texture to the shots," says Tatum.

"Texture?" asks Evan, but Tatum ignores him.

We walk on to the Holiday Village for a quick milkshake in the clubhouse, search online for information about Doug Billings, and check if we've missed anything about Alice and Rose. There are a couple more articles about the discovery of Rose's body, both saying that the autopsy report still hasn't been released, and nothing about Doug apart from facts we already know: he was a solicitor, he was five years older than her and died in 1961, only three years after Rose.

"Doug didn't sound very nice," I say. "I felt sorry for

Alice. Margery made it pretty clear that she rushed into the marriage."

"My money's on Doug and Alice murdering Rose," says Tatum. I realize she's filming. "All I need is the motive. Let's discuss what it might be."

I shake my head. I'm not playing along with her. The other two copy me. Tatum presses the red button. "But this documentary is shaping up so well," she whines.

"You're not including us — not in the right way," I say. "You're just using us."

Tatum snaps, "You don't know what you're talking about. The key to a good investigative documentary is in the editing. I need loads of material to begin with so I have to film as much as I can. And it needs to be exciting, otherwise who cares? I'm not apologizing for being passionate about this project."

"You never know, the documentary might hit on something," says Evan. "The police are never going to be able to spend much time on a murder that happened so long ago, are they? Stretched resources and all that."

"Exactly," says Tatum, pointing at him as if he's her star student.

"Even less time if they think it's a suicide," says Ivy.

"Uh-huh," says Tatum.

"But you're..." I don't know how to explain my misgivings. How I suspect she might have bumped into Ivy on purpose so that Ivy would knock Jakob down the stairs, just to make the prediction about a twist of fate come true. I'm starting to really think she would manipulate anything to get it on film.

"I'm interviewing Poppy this afternoon," says Tatum. "It's all set up. Poppy's agreed."

Ivy and I look at each other.

"I'm going to be there," says Ivy.

"Of course," says Tatum.

Ivy looks at the huge clock on the wall above the reception desk. "We'd better go back for lunch. If Mum's not feeling her best, I'll have to make sure Poppy eats something."

"You want to walk back via Alice's bungalow that she lived in before going into Silverways?" asks Evan.

"Evan!" screeches Tatum. "Why didn't you mention that earlier? Yes, I absolutely want to film the bungalow."

"Don't bother knocking on the door, though," says Evan. "There won't be anyone there. The couple who live there spend the winter in Spain."

"Who needs Neighbourhood Watch with you around?" says Tatum with a wink.

The bungalow isn't on the way back to Roeshot House. We have to do a massive detour, but it's worth it because I'd never have guessed Alice would be happy to live somewhere so different to Roeshot House. It's small, neat and dull, on a cul-de-sac. Tatum films it for a couple of minutes, then says she wants to see the back garden, but the rest of us tell her we should be heading back and she can't climb over the fence or the side gate.

She takes no notice. "It's open," she shouts, trying the side gate. "I won't be long."

"Typical," says Ivy. She looks at her phone. "Mum and Poppy will be wondering where we are."

"You could go back and tell them we're on our way?" I suggest. I feel a lightness in my body, a sudden hopefulness that if Ivy goes and I stay, Evan and I will have a few minutes alone, depending how long Tatum takes in the back garden. "With everything that's gone on and Jakob in hospital, I'm sure they'll be worried. I'll wait for Tatum," I say, sitting on the low brick wall in front of the bungalow.

Ivy nods. I bet she knows what's just gone through my head. "All right. If Mum asks, I'll tell her we were with Evan's friends this morning."

"Thanks," I say. I give her the Amigo salute, only partly as a joke.

Evan sits next to me, leaving a gap between us. It's quite a small gap.

"I hope nobody calls the police to say we're hanging around, or sees Tatum in the back garden," I say.

"Hmm," he says. "Let's hope not." He shifts closer and I can feel the heat of his body against me, although he's not quite touching me.

This is Pinhurst, where – despite a disturbing few days – good things happen. I feel brave enough to say, "I loved the Holiday Village disco."

"It was fun, wasn't it?" says Evan.

It's quiet. No cars, nobody in sight. We can't hear Tatum.

I move my hand until it brushes against his, and then our hands are latched together and my thumb is stroking his skin. I have the sensation of parts of my body being on different speed settings, some slowed down, others speeded up. We swivel towards each other and make eye contact. Awkward, wonderful eye contact. He brings one hand up. It's an exquisite kind of agony waiting for it to touch the back of my neck, and a new kind of pleasure as he moves it up further into my hair.

We hear Tatum shout, "Guess what? There are lots of roses back here!" and Evan brings his hand down. We stand up.

She's fiddling about with the latch on the gate.

"Can you meet later?" Evan asks me.

I don't want Ivy to think I'm abandoning her to look after Poppy on her own, or to make an enemy of Tatum. "It's hard with the others," I say. "But, maybe I could leave the house later this afternoon for a run and meet you?"

"Perfect," he says. "It's a date."

I grin. *A date?*

"Come to my house. The address is in the Roeshot House folder. Any time's fine."

What about your parents?

He reads my mind and adds hastily, "Mum and Dad are visiting some friends today."

Tatum is beside us. "Where's Ivy? No, don't tell me. She rushed back to check on darling Poppy. She needs to let go a little, don't you think?"

TWENTY-TWO

Auntie Gabs is still in bed when we get back. Ivy sighs and explains it as being "one of those days". Poppy says Clive has been round to look at the attic window and the loose carpet on the stair. He's fixed the carpet, and he wants someone else to look at the window to work out how the bar could have become dislodged.

"I told him Mum was asleep but he could come in. That was OK, wasn't it?" says Poppy. Her eyes are big and anxious.

"You probably should have asked him to come back another time, but don't worry," says Ivy. She's put some food on the table, arranging the cheese on a wooden board to look appealing, like her mum would have done. The bread has been warmed up in the oven.

"At least the stair is safe," I say.

Poppy eats her usual tiny amount and Ivy does the usual cajoling. I pick at some carrot sticks and cut myself a thin slice of cheese. There's so much cheese for us to get through. The fruit bowl is overflowing. With only four of us sitting round the table, it feels off-kilter. Tatum takes some ham Ivy has sliced from the big chunk in the fridge and pushes it into a soft piece of bread. As she eats, she watches back footage of Margery with the volume up until I tell her to stop and nod in Poppy's direction.

"Who's that old lady you're speaking to?" asks Poppy.

Too late.

"Evan's grandma," lies Tatum smoothly. "It's for my school project about Pinhurst. People's memories. Interesting things that have happened in the village. Like your ghost."

"Oh," says Poppy.

"Have you seen the ghost again?" Ivy asks.

"No," says Poppy, "but I've been waiting for her."

"Don't tell me about it here," says Tatum, picking up her phone. "I want to interview you properly, but I want the right setting. The conservatory. Good light, and atmospheric with the cracked panes of glass and those knobbly old geraniums."

"How's that atmospheric?" asks Ivy, but Tatum's already on her feet.

"I'll go and set it up," she says, leaving us to put away the lunch things. "Give me five minutes."

"Poppy, you don't have to do the interview," says Ivy.

"I don't mind." Poppy gets up and brings her plate to the dishwasher. Her legs are stiff and she's walking in her strange way.

Ivy and I go with Poppy to the conservatory, where she settles herself on a metal chair. She crosses her legs. Her knees are like bulges and I feel horrible for thinking before that she might be faking her illness.

"Looking good, Pops!" says Ivy. "Don't be nervous."

"I'm not," says Poppy. She glares at her sister.

"Okaaaay," says Tatum. "Now. . ." She presses record. "Please can you tell me about the ghost you saw."

Poppy describes her again. I listen out for the little details to see if they've changed, but they haven't.

"How d'you know the ghost was old if you didn't see her face?" asks Tatum.

"Because she was bent over." Poppy hunches forward to demonstrate. "Her hair was long and grey."

"What was she doing?"

"She was standing by Rose's grave. Looking. Maybe she was talking too."

"Tell us why we should believe you," says Tatum, and Poppy looks confused.

"She was real. I did see her."

"But you didn't touch her?"

"She was outside," says Poppy. "I couldn't touch her." She sounds panicky. "Don't you believe me?"

"Actually, I do believe you," says Tatum. She's not

looking at her screen any more but directly at Poppy. "I'm not surprised at all that you saw a ghost."

Poppy's face relaxes.

"What d'you think the ghost wants?" asks Tatum conversationally.

"I'm . . . I'm not sure," says Poppy. "She was just there."

"I think Alice is worried," says Tatum. "Her sister is out for revenge. Terrible things are happening, aren't they? Baz . . . Jakob. . ."

So slowly it's not noticeable at first, Poppy shrinks away from Tatum.

Tatum lowers her voice. "Why d'you think you're the only one who's seen her?"

Poppy blinks nervously. "I don't know."

"Are you like Alice? Do you have secrets too?"

Poppy emits a high-pitched sob. It skewers me and has Ivy rushing towards her sister.

"Stop filming, Tatum," says Ivy. "That's enough. You're scaring her."

TWENTY-THREE

I wait until Poppy is settled on the sofa with Ivy looking through magazines before I get changed into running gear. Tatum is in our room, looking over the footage of her interrogation with Poppy.

"Why did you have to be so cruel?" I ask as I quickly take off my jeans and pull on my leggings.

Tatum says, "She's not a baby. She's the one who wants the attention."

"So you don't believe her, even though you said you did?"

Tatum raises an eyebrow. "I'm keeping an open mind. If you ask me, with this weird house, anything is possible." I turn my back to change into a sport bra and rummage in my suitcase for a T-shirt. My hoodie is half under the bed. I slide it back out and put it on.

"Tatum?" I say at the door. "How did Jakob fall last night?"

"Ivy tripped on the loose carpet." She gives me a direct look. "Why? You were there too. What d'you think happened?"

"Did you film it?"

She shakes her head. "Despite what you think, I don't film absolutely everything."

"Just ... the twist of fate prediction," I say, as I do up the zip of my hoodie. "It's ... scary." I'm not brave enough to tell her it was also very convenient for her documentary, and I think she might have had something to do with it.

Tatum nods vigorously. "Yep, it's scary." She runs her finger across her lip a couple of times. "I must put on some lip balm. My lips have got so dry. I tell you, this house is bad for my health."

"I'm going for a run," I say, picking up my running shoes. I'll put them on somewhere else; I don't like being on my own with her any more than I have to – it's as if she enjoys making me feel uneasy.

"Hang on, Leah. What's up with your aunt? Why's she taken to her bed like somebody in a costume drama?"

"She has days like this," I say. "Since my uncle died. Although I thought she was over them, because last year it seemed as if she was back to normal. She'll probably be all right tomorrow."

"I didn't know Ivy's family was such a bunch of oddballs," Tatum says. "I might not have come here if I'd known." She climbs under her duvet. "Enjoy your run."

I go into the bathroom, brush my teeth and check my face in the mirror. No truly horrific spots. I think about borrowing Tatum's mascara, but use my own slightly dried-up one instead, in case she notices, then I lace my running shoes and go downstairs to take a quick photo of Evan's address from the house folder in the hallway. It feels like sneaky, un-Amigo-like behaviour, but it's easier not to say anything to Ivy, not before I've actually done this anyway. My stomach gurgles, unsettled. I look through the kitchen blinds before I leave. The sky is marbled white and grey like a kitchen worktop, and the temperature's dropped. I take my hat and scarf from my coat. Gloves will be a pain so I'll pull my hoodie sleeves over my hands.

I yell goodbye to Ivy and run to the end of the drive. As soon as I'm out of sight and I have a signal, I stop and search Evan's address on my maps app, memorizing the route. I check for a message from Jakob, but there's nothing. I take a selfie looking sad, with *"Missing You"* at the bottom. Before I send it, I add *"LOTS"*, then *"Please tell me you're OK"*.

It's good to run and have some time away from the others to think. I'm not sure Roeshot House will ever be the same for me again now I know its secret. Memories of Baz's death and Jakob's fall won't fade anytime soon either. Cold air stings the back of my throat as I pick up my pace and forget to close my mouth for a few seconds. I like the rhythm of my running shoes on the pavement. It helps to block out the swell of anger against Tatum and my increasing worry about what she might do next.

As I turn into Evan's road, I slow down, nervous. It's more rural than Donna's road, with farmland interspersed between houses, and none of them alike. Evan's house is like a series of outbuildings which have been glued together. There's a skip in the drive and a couple of long ladders chained together down the side. A cat sits in an empty birdbath in the overgrown front garden.

I hesitate outside his front door and then, as if it's red-hot, I push the doorbell. The door opens almost straight away and he's there.

"Hey! Come in."

I step into his blissfully warm house. I can feel the underfloor heating even before I've taken off my running shoes. I remove my hat, scarf and hoodie and leave them in a clothes puddle in the hallway to stay warm for my return journey, my mobile on top.

We walk into a large but cluttered kitchen. All the surfaces are covered with misshapen pottery vases, wooden bowls, photos and jars of dried food.

"I make the wooden bowls," says Evan. "Mum does the pottery. Her pieces are wonky on purpose, by the way."

By the oven there are three wooden bowls, nestling one inside the other. I pick up the smallest. It's completely smooth, the colour of cooked pastry, with all the gradations from golden brown to almost burnt.

"I like carving birds best," says Evan. He lifts a round little wooden bird from a cluttered shelf on the dresser. "This is my wren."

I take it from him, holding it carefully in the palm of my hand, its tiny little feet super-delicate. "I don't know what a wren looks like, but this is impressive," I say. "You know Steve, who we think ran over Baz and didn't own up? He paints birds. On little canvases. He spends *hours* on them. He paints like this. . ."

I scrunch my shoulders and screw-up my face. Evan grins at my unflattering but entirely accurate impression. "I love carving things. It's way more satisfying than putting up shelves and all the boring jobs Dad wants me to do."

"My dad's hopeless at anything practical." I wish I hadn't said that. I don't want to think about Dad now.

I hand back the wren, while Evan reaches for teabags and mugs. I lean against the work surface and tell him how different Pinhurst is to where I live. I describe the sea wall, with the waves crashing below our feet, the Fish 'n' Chip Shack, the fat seagulls and the things we find at low tide. Shoes and polished stones, plastic buckets turned white by the sea and once a whole rusty bicycle.

Evan moves away to fetch milk from the fridge. He pours it into the mugs and hands me one. "I still haven't had breakfast yet. D'you want a pancake?"

"Sure," I say, though my body's on too high alert to contemplate eating.

He gathers the ingredients for a pancake batter, and before he makes it, he chops up a banana, pours some chopped nuts into a bowl, stands on a chair to locate a jar of Nutella at the back of a cupboard, finds an almost-finished maple syrup bottle and turns it upside down, cuts a lemon in half and flicks the pips at me, and spoons out the manky bits from the sugar bowl on the table. He makes the batter effortlessly, without a recipe.

I move next to the hob to watch him pour the mixture into a pan. The first pancake fails and ends up as unappetizing lump. "It's times like this we need a dog," says Evan as he dumps it into the food waste bin. "Sorry," he says, stricken. "I shouldn't have said that. That was insensitive."

"It's OK," I say.

"You know, I regret saying that about the cars and Baz. Now you're convinced it's Steve's fault and it might have been a delivery van, or even someone turning around in the driveway."

"But it's likely to have been him, isn't it?" I say.

"It's a possibility. Listen: the next pancake is going to be awesome, yeah?"

I watch him pour the mixture. It firms up much more quickly than the first. It definitely looks more like a pancake.

"Stand back," says Evan. He flips it high and catches it perfectly. "Whoa. Class act. This is yours." He slides the pancake on to a plate and hands it to me.

I add some Nutella and banana and take a couple of bites as he makes two more pancakes, piling them up on a plate. He squeezes lemon over the top one, then scatters sugar, rolls it to the width of a marker pen and eats it.

"You want a turn?" he asks, pushing the pan handle towards me.

I'm unprepared for the breath-catch in my throat as I swirl the batter into the pan: the last time I made pancakes was in our old house with Dad, before he left and life changed. Dad was all about squeezed lemon and sugar. "Simple pleasures," he'd say. Now, with Amber wanting a baby, me not knowing half the time if I want to see him or not and his job looking precarious, his life is far from simple.

"Nice," says Evan. "But the real test is in the flipping."

"Of course," I say. "You want to see pancake flipping? Watch this!" I check the pancake is loose, before gripping the handle with both hands. With a quick upward movement, I send the pancake flying. It doesn't go quite as high as I was expecting but it lands like a dream. "Pretty good, hmm?"

"We can do better," says Evan, and I don't clock his use of "we" until I've added that pancake to the pile, and I slug another lot of batter in the pan. "Joint effort," he says, and he takes my hands and places them with his on the handle.

He leans against me. I smell the duvet scent of him, oil in a pan, the sharpness of the lemon on the table. His hands feel warm against mine.

"OK, ready?" He lifts the pan and I'm expecting him to count three but he doesn't. He flings the pan upwards and slightly backwards, but I'm not ready. My body falls back against his, and the pancake pirouettes to the ceiling and comes hurtling towards my head. I yelp, and move back, but Evan moves forward to catch the pancake, which flops over the side of the pan, half in, half out, and I'm wedged uncomfortably between the oven and Evan with an arm that's been yanked too far out of its socket.

I let go of the pan at the same time as Evan. It crashes on to the hob.

He spins me round. "I'm so sorry. Did I hurt you?" He sees me rubbing the top of my arm. "Have you pulled something? Oh, God. Sorry."

"I'll live," I say. I think he trod on my foot too, and my hip is sore from hitting the side of the oven.

He steps away to assess me. "Sure?"

I'm suddenly conscious of the tightness of my leggings, the T-shirt that's ridden up. "Sure," I say, pulling down my T-shirt. I hope I don't have globs of pancake batter in my hair.

He's holding my gaze and I know what he's asking.

I reply by taking a step forward. I lift my head ever so slightly and relax my lips. So slowly it's twitchingly painful, he lowers his mouth on to mine, and we kiss. Properly kiss, so that I taste lemony pancake sweetness and breakfast tea. Every sensuous nerve ending throughout my body is on fire. Every thought is channelled into my tongue and lips, and this soft, closed-eye magic. When I break away to breathe, I laugh and he laughs at me laughing. It takes me by surprise, this outpouring of bursting happiness.

We kiss again, and I think I'm a natural. When we break off, I'm about to say this, but there's the sound of someone coming downstairs.

"Oh, great," says Evan with heavy sarcasm. "It's Lily, my sister. She works shifts at the pub."

I spring away as his sister comes into the kitchen in a big pink dressing gown, yawning noisily. She's an older but shorter version of Evan, with a great deal more wavy hair, which is mostly up in a springy ponytail. She has a tiny glittery nose piercing and smudged eyeliner under one eye.

"Oh, hi!" says Lily. "I didn't know you had someone here, Ev. Sorry. Hi! Oooh, pancakes. Any going spare?"

"Here." Evan holds out the plate. "This is Leah. She's staying at Roeshot House."

"Cheers," says Lily. "Hello, Leah."

"Hi. I should be getting back," I say.

"Don't mind me," says Lily. "I'm half-asleep. It was busy last night. Oh – but I heard some insider gossip from someone involved in the Alice Billings case."

My skin prickles.

"And?" says Evan.

"It seems Rose's injuries are, and I quote, 'consistent with someone falling to their death'."

TWENTY-FOUR

"So it was suicide?" says Evan.

"Or she was pushed," says Lily. "She probably fell from the roof."

"I reckon it was the attic," I say. That window. The metal bar across it, so that it couldn't happen again. The burial spot nearby. "She could have climbed on to the window seat and got on to the outside ledge."

"Oh, yeah," says Lily. "You could be right. That makes a lot of sense. I'm going to tell the group chat." She sits down at the table and fiddles with her phone.

"Poor Rose," I say. I picture her standing precariously on the ledge, stretching her arms out and contemplating the fall. I think of the triangulation column on Chandler's

Hill. That sense of letting go. But something feels off. It doesn't fit with the photos of the exuberant teenager we saw. But, of course, it's impossible to know what's going on under the surface.

Evan traces his finger up the inside of my arm and, although it tickles, it's also the best sensation ever. "Can't you stay a bit longer?" he asks.

I look at the clock display on the oven. "Five minutes?"

He tugs my hand. "I want to show you the workshop. Come with me."

Lily shoots me an amused look. "An invitation to the workshop! Watch out."

"Oi!" says Evan, and he swipes at her head as we go past, but she ducks in time. "The workshop's in the garage. There's a door through here. Put on those ugly clog things of Mum's; there might be bits on the floor."

I notice he doesn't bother to put on shoes himself.

The garage is fitted out like a proper workshop. There are three workbenches, a shelving unit, and stacks of wood, huge pieces, down to small logs.

"I want to show you something," says Evan. He picks his way over the floor, avoiding occasional curls of shaved wood. He indicates that I should sit on a chair.

I sit on it then stand up again to take a closer look. "Did you make this?" It looks like something you'd see in a posh, bespoke furniture shop: smaller than your average chair, the back made up of two upwards struts and three curved sections going across.

"Yep, my first chair. That's not what I want to show you, but you might not want to sit down on it too hard."

"Er... OK." I lower myself down in a controlled squat sort of a way.

He takes a piece of paper from a shelf and passes it to me. "I printed this off the internet when I got back from Margery's." It's a photo of a blue-painted birdhouse with a black roof and a bar for birds to perch on. "I liked the design. I thought I could paint a rose on the side. Attach it somewhere close to where Rose was buried."

"That would be perfect," I say. "I love it. Your dad couldn't object to a birdhouse." I hand the piece of paper back to him. "How long will it take to make?"

"Not long. I'll ping a photo over to you when it's finished."

I won't see it properly, though – or Evan – until next New Year. It's a sad thought. I stand up. Ivy and Tatum will wonder where I've got to.

"I'll walk you back to Roeshot House," says Evan.

Back to the strange atmosphere of Jakob being gone, Auntie Gabs hiding herself away, Ivy obsessing over Poppy, and Tatum... "I hope you don't think I'm being weird," I say, as I layer up with my hoodie in the hall and he puts on his trainers, "but what d'you think of Tatum?"

He raises his eyebrows. "Er . . . she seems OK. Why?"

"She makes me feel uncomfortable. She doesn't care

what she says or does. I think she might have somehow made Jakob fall downstairs."

"It wasn't the carpet, then?" He takes a jacket from a hook and puts it on.

"Yes, but... I don't know," I admit. "But I know she craves the drama. She wants it for her documentary. She threw up when she saw Baz, but she was a little bit excited too."

"Ew. She's your aunt's friend's daughter, right?" confirms Evan. "Not a complete stranger?"

I shake my head as I bend down to lace my running shoes. "But Ivy didn't know her, and my Auntie Gabs can be flaky. I don't know why I'm telling you... Just, if anything else strange happens, I've told someone."

I look up. He's making an over-the-top alarmed face. "That sounds dramatic!"

"Sorry. She's winding me up, that's what it is." I bounce up. "I'm ready."

After he pulls the front door behind us, I take his hand and place it in the fleece-lined pocket of my hoodie.

We walk fast to keep warm, but when Roeshot House is visible, we slow. "I'll say goodbye here," I say when we reach the driveway. "It's easier."

"All right," says Evan, but he doesn't remove his hand. Our breath, visible in the cold, mingles as we talk.

"This has been so nice," I say.

Evan smiles. He finally takes his hand away and encircles me with his arms, and we kiss. I plant smaller kisses over his face. He touches my cold-numb cheek with the tips of his fingers and they come alive. I should go. I know I should go.

"Bye, then," I say and don't move.

"Bye, then," he says. "I'll come by tomorrow before you go," and he kisses me one last lingering time before I force myself to pull away.

TWENTY-FIVE

"*Someone* was lying about going running!" says Tatum when I walk into the kitchen.

"You and Evan were going for it out there," says Ivy, amazed.

My heart jumps, as if I've been caught doing something bad. "You were *watching*?"

"I looked out of the window and there you were," says Tatum. "In full view. You obviously wanted us to see, so don't pretend to get defensive."

I'm an idiot, and Tatum has good eyesight.

"Did you arrange to meet Evan?" asks Ivy. She looks hurt.

"I . . . told him I might go for a run this afternoon," I say.

"Riiiiight," says Tatum.

"I'm sorry," I say to Ivy. "I felt awkward about it."

"First kiss!" sings Tatum. "Big moment!"

Ivy says she understands, but that makes me feel worse. If Tatum weren't here Ivy'd be asking me everything about Evan, and I'd be telling her. If Jakob were here, he'd be beside himself with excitement.

Jakob. I hate not knowing how he is. I hate him not being here.

Ivy opens the cupboard next to the oven, where the baking trays and tins are kept. She takes out two trays. "Poppy's asked to make cookies. We brought the ingredients with us, and some funky cutters. You want to help?" She nods towards various packets. Coconut sugar. Non-dairy butter.

"Of course," I say.

"Evan's cute," says Ivy. "It's a shame you're leaving tomorrow and live so far away."

Tatum says, "Have you noticed he smells of bonfires?"

"No he doesn't. But anyway, I like the smell of bonfires," I say.

Tatum raises an eyebrow.

I was going to tell her the gossip about Rose's injuries, but after what Tatum said about Evan, she doesn't deserve to know. I take off my scarf and hat, and wonder if I'll ever be happy sitting in the attic again, knowing it's probably where Rose fell from.

"Have you accepted you're the unlucky-in-love person yet?" asks Tatum "I'm just looking out for you: you need to see this for what it is. As soon as you've gone, Evan will hook up with the next available girl who flirts with him. You'll come back next year and it'll be hideously embarrassing. He'll avoid you, and you'll wonder what you ever saw in him."

"Leah will be going out with someone else by then," says Ivy loyally – I think.

Tatum smiles. "Who knows?"

"I'm not interested in what you think," I say, less calmly than I'd have liked.

"You're so naïve, Leah."

"And you're..." I search for the right words. "You're just jealous because you liked Evan. Stop talking about the predictions. You weren't even there when we made them. You're taking them out of context and making everything weird for your precious documentary. You're pathetic."

"Everything was already weird, Leah," says Tatum. "That's what you haven't quite grasped yet." She goes out to the corridor and slams the kitchen door.

Ivy and I look at each other.

"She better not be here next year," I say. "Or Steve."

"You were right about her being jealous of Evan," says Ivy. She lifts a wooden spoon out of the utensil pot on the kitchen counter. "She seemed kind of upset when she first saw you two through the window. So maybe don't go on about him in front of her. It winds her up."

"I promise I didn't think anyone could see us there."

"I know, but be careful."

"What d'you mean, 'Be careful'?" I ask.

Ivy looks round. The door to the lounge and the door to the corridor are both closed.

"What's Tatum said?"

"Thing is, I'm pretty sure she came here intent on stirring things up. She wanted to do a documentary and she needs it to be as stand-out as possible. For film school."

"What d'you mean?"

"When I went upstairs to check on Mum she asked how we were getting on. Obviously I told her we were all fine. Then she said something about Tatum's mum telling her Tatum had a big project to be getting on with, so at least she has that to keep her busy. That must be the documentary. Tatum's not been doing any school stuff since she's been here, has she?"

"Nope." I've not seen a book in Tatum's hand apart from the Roeshot garden one. "But maybe she told her mum about everything that's been going on?"

"No, my mum said her mum told her that *before* we got here."

I stare at her, my heart thumping. Tatum seriously lucked out with us. A dead body in the garden. Predictions.

"I didn't want to say this, but I think she somehow knocked into me when I got to the stair with the loose carpet, which meant I had to step back into Jakob," says Ivy.

"That's what I thought too," I say. "She might have killed him." My brain is making connections. "That metal bar. D'you think she had anything to do with that? Should we ... say something?"

"To her?"

"No, to Auntie Gabs," I say.

"We don't have any proof, so it's just going to make more drama. Mum's not up to that right now."

The door from the lounge opens and we jump apart. It's Poppy. I wonder how much she heard.

"I thought you said we were going to make cookies," she says.

Ivy pins on a smile. "We are, Popster. Look, Leah and I've been getting everything ready."

Poppy weighs the ingredients but we have to help her mix the dough as it needs more strength than she's got. She rolls it out and the three of us cut out shapes, making scenes on the baking trays, with palm trees, boats, fish and monsters.

I wonder what Tatum is doing. Reviewing her footage, no doubt, and dreaming up the next part of her film. Maybe the focus of it isn't on Alice and Rose at all, but on hysteria, or gullibility, or something.

We eat little scraps of leftover dough. It tastes as if it needs more sugar, but I'm not going to say that. I make a show of saying how much I love it, and Ivy smiles gratefully at me.

While we wait for the biscuits to cool, Poppy has a

milkshake and Ivy and I make the different-coloured icings. Poppy describes a film she's heard of but can't remember the title. I try to guess. Ivy doesn't join in. She carefully works in tiny drops of food colouring to the little bowls of white icing I've made. I wonder how much she gets to go out and have fun when she's home, and how many things she has to cancel if Auntie Gabs has "one of her days".

Poppy spends ages decorating the cookies while Ivy and I prepare a salad for later to go with some leftover lasagne from the fridge, because she says Auntie Gabs won't be in a cooking mood. We talk about Jakob, wondering how he's doing, and our mood is subdued. Outside the light turns pale and expectant, as if it might snow. I go to the window to close the blinds, thinking about Tatum seeing me kiss Evan. I have a flutter of anxiety in my chest and wish Evan were here now.

"Come up to the attic with me, Ivy," I say, turning away from the curtains. "Please? Just for five minutes."

She gives me an odd look but she tells Poppy we'll be right back. We run up there, not treading on the stair Jakob tripped on, even though Clive has nailed the carpet carefully back into place. We creep past my room, where Tatum must be behind the closed door, and up into the attic.

I walk to the window and tell Ivy that it's possible Rose jumped from the ledge, and she steps back, then forward to imagine Rose, like I did, standing there before she fell. How long did she wait? Could someone have saved her?

Ivy sits on the window seat and says softly, "Have you ever thought of jumping?"

I scan her face. She's serious. "No," I say. "Not that sort of a jump." I'm scared to ask her, but I do. "You?"

She nods. "Only once. But looking after Poppy and Mum is hard."

The prediction about something of great value being lost comes into my mind, and it occurs to me that perhaps it's not a concrete thing like binoculars, but something like hope, or trust.

And I think about Poppy's prediction.

"You do an amazing job," I say. I wish I knew what else to say. I bet Jakob would find the right words if he was here, but he's not, so I hug her and say, "I'm so sorry."

Gabs gets out of bed for dinner. She apologizes for being out of it, blaming it on a new medication. She's wearing the same dress that she wore for New Year's Eve, with the impractical sleeves, except now it's creased and has a stain down the front. It's pretty clear that she's in bad shape, much worse than last year. I doubt Mum would have left me here, if she'd known about this. She walks slowly to the end of the drive with her phone, and returns saying that Elaine and Marc are staying the night in a Premier Inn near the hospital, and won't be back until Jakob's had his second operation.

Ivy has laid the table and made everything look nice with the decorated cookies as a centrepiece, but it feels dismal without Jakob. Tatum is sulking, and Poppy colours her nails with black Sharpie. She says her mouth and stomach are on fire, so Ivy crushes ice-cubes for her to suck.

"Our last night," says Auntie Gabs. "We usually have a big board games marathon," she says to Tatum, "but perhaps we're not in the mood." She presses her forehead. "Elaine is good at organizing that, and my head isn't up to it."

"It's fine, Mum," says Ivy. "We don't want to play board games."

"Too freaking right," mutters Tatum.

Ivy collects the plates and I stand to help her.

"It's been a very tiring few days, hasn't it?" says Auntie Gabs.

"Jakob had an idea, Auntie Gabs," I say. "He thought Poppy could stay with his family for a change of scene. When he's better. That might be a while, I guess." I don't mention the doctor part, and I don't say anything about giving her and Ivy a break because Poppy is sitting right there. I should have picked a better time to do this. "Mum and I would love to have her come and stay too sometime."

Through a mouthful of ice, Poppy says, "Yes, please."

"You'd have to write out the food things, but we'd manage," I say to Auntie Gabs.

"What a nice idea, thank you," Auntie Gabs says. "We could have a think about that, couldn't we, Pops?"

Ivy ruffles the top of Poppy's head, and I see Ivy's right: Poppy's hair has become much thinner. "I guess it's doable if we plan it far enough ahead."

Poppy reaches for my hand and colours my thumbnail black. "I'd like to be with Leah," she whispers, and the evening doesn't feel like quite such a disaster.

TWENTY-SIX

My phone says 3:14 a.m. I don't know what's woken me, but there's a squawking outside, so it might have been that. The bird's call is insistent. When I look over at Tatum, I can make out her body rising and falling in time with her breathing.

We hardly spoke to each other when we went to bed. She was looking yet again at the footage she'd shot, with earphones in, and I watched her eyes dart back and forth. That documentary is everything to her, like an addictive game.

I try to conjure up the floaty feeling I had with Evan, but I'm cold and lonely. Thoughts intrude about Mum and Steve coming back with An Announcement. Knowing there are only five of us sleeping in Roeshot House tonight makes me nervous, especially when the only adult isn't fully functioning. Ironically, it's what we Amigos always longed for: a house with zero adult interference. I picture Jakob in a hospital bed, recovering from one operation, facing another. I wonder if he's awake too.

Do I smell roses? My stomach churns. I do. I'm sure I do. Or is it my imagination?

I mustn't think about it. I'll think about next New Year, which will be better. Tatum won't be with us, and we won't be so obsessed with Alice and Rose. The doctors will have found a way to treat Poppy, Jakob will be OK, and Ivy will be fun again and less stressed about Poppy. Evan will still fancy me one year on. I lean down for the bed socks I discarded earlier and put them on again. I pull the duvet tight around me, trapping a layer of warm air.

I drift off to sleep, but I lurch awake, slicked with sweat, as if I have a high temperature.

Rose. I dreamt she was screaming for help. I heard a scuffle, but I didn't know where she was. I ran into different rooms in Roeshot House, but they were empty.

Somehow I knew a baby was going to die and I couldn't do anything about it. I climbed the stairs to the attic and I squeezed through the window on to a ledge. I took another step and fell.

I reach for my phone: 5:38 a.m. A car roars along the road at the end of the drive, the sound out of place. It makes me think of Baz. The only way to stop myself thinking about him – and the person who ran him over – is to get up. By the time I've gone to the toilet, I'm wide awake. What would it be like to go running now? I go to the window and yank the curtain aside.

What is that? *Who* is that? Beyond the car, standing by the burial site, is a figure with long white-silver hair, in a shapeless white garment. A ghost.

Poppy's ghost.

My ribs press inwards and stop me breathing. I am completely, painfully aware of every part of my body reacting to the fear: there's a strange noise in my ears like the swishing of blood, and my heart is bouncing out of control.

I blink and the ghost is still there. I don't understand what I'm seeing. Although I can't see her face, she looks real, but her dress is thin and her feet are bare and she appears unaware of the cold. Her skin is whitish-blue, her limbs fragile.

I reach for my phone on the bedside table, take frantic photos for a couple of seconds. I want to see her expression. Is it sorrowful or gleeful? For a moment, I'm paralyzed by the window, torn between waiting and watching, and the urge to run downstairs and outside.

"Tatum?" I say. Then louder. "Tatum, wake up." I prod her, while still keeping an eye on the ghost.

Tatum rolls towards me and swears.

"There's a ghost. It's Poppy's ghost."

"There is no ghost. Leave me alone. Go back to sleep."

I take a couple more photos then tussle into a sweatshirt and jam my bed-socked feet into my trainers. I tie the laces too tightly, but there's no time to redo them.

Rushing back to the window to check one last time before I run downstairs, I see the woman turn towards the gates at the end of the drive, as if she's leaving. I skitter down the stairs, taking a few at a time, half-stumbling, half-springing. The front door is locked with a key that turns easily, but there's the security chain to navigate. It takes a few goes to open with shaky fingers.

The crisp air startles me, shocks me into taking a bigger breath than I need to. I can't see the woman. She's melted away, as I feared she would. I run to the end of the drive and I look up the road. Nobody to be seen. There are two side roads, though – she had time to vanish down them.

"Nooo," I say out loud, and a bird flies out of a tree nearby, wings flapping too close. I crouch instinctively, hyper-alert.

But lower to the ground, I see very faint footprints that peter out to the right of the entrance. I follow them backwards to the grass, where they are firmer, and here there are two sets, one leading to the site, and another back towards the gate. Human feet pressing down on grass, picking up the dew, and leaving damp prints on the concrete drive for a bit. Bare human feet in winter?

I don't want to trawl the eerie early morning Pinhurst

streets half-dressed, so I go back inside. Tatum is still asleep, making muttering noises as if she's dreaming.

My trainers are hard to force off my feet because I've done them up so tightly, but as soon as they're off, I huddle under the duvet. In the dark, I check my phone. *There are photos.* I have seven shots of a blurred figure in a dress. Evidence.

I enlarge each photo to big fuzzy pixels. I've occasionally seen photos with alleged ghosts posted online. They usually turn out to be superimposed photos or shadows, or objects that combine to make a face. Why would someone stand next to the grave with no shoes and a flimsy dress in the middle of winter? There's no logical explanation.

Has Tatum set me up? Am I part of an elaborate prank?

TWENTY-SEVEN

There's something hard under my hip when I wake up: my phone. It's just gone nine o'clock. I look across at Tatum's bed. She's not there. I check the photos of the ghost are still on my phone – I didn't make her up . . . so neither did Poppy.

I get up and look out of the window. No ghost. The official checkout time today is four o'clock, but I can't see Clive making too much of a fuss if we're later; I doubt anyone else has booked the house anytime soon. Mum and Steve's arrival depends on the road conditions up north, and Elaine and Marc won't want to race back for their belongings until after Jakob's operation. As soon as I've had some breakfast, I'll go down the drive to check my messages. I really hope there's one from Jakob. And Evan.

Last days at Roeshot House have always been the same up until now. A walk to Porrit's Corner. Hot chocolates in the cafe there. Thoughts of going back to school. The feeling of a good time coming to an end.

Not this year. I add a few more layers of clothing before going downstairs.

"All right?" asks Ivy. She's in the kitchen putting things into a plastic crate. Tatum and Poppy are sitting at the table, doing a puzzle with matchsticks. "Mum's not feeling too bright still, so I'm packing up the stuff we won't need for lunch. I'm not sure who's going to be here for lunch, though."

"No one's worried about lunch," I say, dropping a slice of toast into the toaster, but then I regret being so flippant. Ivy's doing her best to keep the show on the road. "Let me know what you want help with," I say.

Tatum flicks her eyes up at me. "Leah, see these four squares? Make three equal-size squares moving just three matchsticks."

I stare at the squares. "Nope, can't see it."

"Mmmmm," says Tatum, as though I've confirmed what she suspected.

Poppy strikes a match from the matchstick box and blows it out. "I don't want to go home," she says.

"Neither do I," I lie. I sit down next to her and bring up the photos. "Poppy," I say. "Is this the ghost you saw the other day?"

She scoops my phone up in both hands and peers. "Yes," she says, her mouth partially open. "Yes! It is! You saw her – that's Alice." She looks at me with relief. "I told you. I wasn't making it up."

Tatum and Ivy are right beside her now, wanting to see, asking me for an explanation, Tatum demanding to know why I didn't wake her up. She doesn't remember me trying to. "That's so creepy," she murmurs looking over Poppy's shoulder. "She looks really evil."

Ivy enlarges the photo and says, "It's an old lady."

"Give it to me," says Tatum. She snatches the phone and makes the photo normal size again. "Text me these later for backup, yeah? But it'll look more authentic if I film them on your phone for now."

Ivy says, "Oh my God, Tatum," but Tatum is already filming, talking about a confirmed sighting of Poppy's ghost, believed to be Alice.

I swipe my phone back. "Why was an old lady wearing a shift dress and no shoes?" I ask as I enlarge the photo again. "In the cold. In the middle of the night."

"It's an old lady in a nightie," says Ivy.

"Let's see." Tatum makes a big show of looking more closely and says, "Oh dear. Ivy's right. You've confused a mad old woman with a ghost."

Of course. I understand now. Silverways is within easy walking distance. I remember the note on the back of the porch door of Silverways about a woman not being allowed out on her own.

"So not an *actual* ghost, then," I say, deliberately echoing the predictions.

"Not this one," says Tatum, unfazed. "But it's intriguing."

I butter my toast and as I eat it standing up I think about what she said last night when I tried to wake her up. *There is no ghost.* However groggy she was, she didn't believe in Poppy's ghost for one moment. Does that mean she's been making the predictions come true?

Still. Within a few hours I'll never have to see Tatum again.

I go to the fridge to get some juice and hear someone running up the driveway. My stomach flips, hoping it's Evan, but when I reach the window I see it's a young boy in a woollen hat with a rolled-up newspaper. There's an adult at the end of the driveway with a bag on a trolley thing. The boy runs towards the porch with what must be the *Pinhurst and Riddingham Gazette*.

"I'll be back in a minute," I say, leaving the warmth of the kitchen for the cheerless corridor.

The newspaper is lying face down on the mat. When I pick it up, it's slightly damp from being outside. I turn it over and see the headline *Dead girl in garden latest: Rose was PREGNANT.*

I shiver. That dream I had last night. How did I know there was a baby involved?

There's a photo of Rose that we haven't seen before. I wonder if it was found among Alice's things, or if it was supplied by her son. Rose is looking straight into the camera, laughing, the sort of person who seizes life, who you wouldn't be able to tear your eyes from. I skim

read the article. *Rose Strathmortimer was four or five months'
pregnant at the time of her death. She had injuries consistent with
a fall from a significant height. She is believed to have been in the
care of her sister and brother-in-law for the previous six months.*

I take the newspaper to the kitchen and leave it on the
counter so the other two can look at it without Poppy seeing.

But it doesn't even occur to Tatum to keep it on the
down-low. She gasps and says in a loud voice, "Pregnant
at sixteen and not married. Scandal! And omigod, she
jumped!" She sits with it at the table, where Poppy reads
over her shoulder and asks what an inquest is.

"An investigation," says Ivy, annoyed. "Take the paper
away, Tatum."

I shouldn't have brought it into the kitchen. I should
have taken it up to the attic, or even to my bedroom.

Tatum says, "OK. I need to film someone reading out
the article on camera. Any volunteers?"

Ivy and I give her stony looks.

"Do you want to do it, Poppy?" asks Tatum.

"Of course she doesn't want to do it," I say.

Poppy says, "I don't mind. I'm good at reading out
aloud and acting."

"That's what I thought," says Tatum. "Let's go into the
lounge, Poppy. We'll do it there, near the fire. We'll make
it sound like a ghost story."

"No, stay here, Poppy," says Ivy.

Poppy doesn't know what to do, so she brings her head
down to her folded arms on the table.

"She can make her own mind up," says Tatum. "Or isn't that allowed?" She tilts her head on one side, questioningly.

Ivy clenches her jaw. "It's allowed, but I'm watching."

Tatum sighs. "Suit yourself. This way, Miss Poppy."

Ivy and I stand in the doorway between the kitchen and the lounge. Poppy sits on the little stool by the fire, and reads the article fluently and clearly. It's creepy hearing such a hard-hitting article being read out by a small, innocent-sounding kid. When she's finished, she looks up and smiles at Tatum, wanting her approval. She gets it.

"That was perfection," says Tatum.

"I feel sorry for Rose," says Poppy. "I don't think Alice and her husband did a very good job of looking after her."

"I know, right?" says Tatum. "I think I'm going to turn this school project I'm doing into a campaign. Hashtag Justice for Rose. You think that would be good?" I can't tell if she's making fun of Poppy.

Poppy nods solemnly. I know Tatum is still filming. It's sickening. I can't stay here another minute.

"You know what?" I say to Ivy. "I'm going to Silverways. I'm going to find out what that lady was doing here by the grave."

Ivy nods. "I'll stay here and keep an eye on Poppy."

The footsteps from the old lady ghost have long since evaporated. I lean against the wall and check my messages. Jakob has finally got in touch and sent me and Ivy a photo of him with his arm in a cast. The operation on his leg is scheduled for this afternoon. His face is scabbed from where it came into contact with the glass. He's looking glum, an exaggerated sort of glum, for the photo, but if it's meant to make me smile, it doesn't. *Still alive* is the caption. I tell him how worried I've been and wish him luck for this afternoon. Evan's sent me a dancing pancake gif, and says he'll be round this morning when his dad lets him have a break, and I reply with laughing face and a heart. I find him on Instagram, quickly glance through his photos of campfires, artistic log piles, tractors, drinking with friends and some of his carvings, and follow him.

There's a message from Mum saying she and Steve are setting off mid-morning but they'll be taking it slow, and could I make sure I've packed in good time. I Snapchat Sophia and say I have a lot to tell her when I get home.

The village is quiet, still in holiday mode, with some outdoor fairy lights switched on in the gloomy daylight. I walk past a man sitting on a wall with a cigarette. Further along two women with pushchairs walking side by side, blocking the pavement, stare at me as I step on to the road to let them pass.

I wonder what this place was like when Rose was here. How easy was it for her to sneak out of Roeshot House and meet the father of her baby? I imagine exuberant, beautiful Rose's shock at finding out she was pregnant. Margery said she was unconventional – I wonder if she ever imagined herself keeping the baby.

Did she tell her sister? Is that when everything went wrong?

Knocking on the door of an old people's home and asking if one of their residents has been wandering about in the early hours in only a nightie isn't like anything I've done before. I ring the bell and hope it's Donna who opens the door. It's not, but neither is it the lady who gave us the brochure, who thought we were interested in work experience. It's a man with a pierced lip and a navy-blue uniform tunic. He steps into the porch and opens the outer door.

"Morning," he says.

I take a deep breath and get straight to the point, saying I thought I saw a ghost in my garden but I realized it was an elderly person with no shoes and he cuts in and says, "Oh dear. That sounds like Mrs Lupin. She must have broken her new window lock and climbed out. My shift started a few minutes ago so I haven't seen her yet. Thanks for letting us know. I'll look into it."

He goes to close the door, but I say, "If she's awake, d'you think I could have a word with her? Just for five or ten minutes? I want to ask her if she knows anything about the house I'm staying in. I think she's wandered there before."

The man weighs this up a moment.

"I know Donna," I add. "And I'm staying in Alice Billings's old house. Mrs Lupin was standing by where the girl was buried."

"I'd need to check," he says. "It might be nice for Mrs Lupin to have some company, although I'd have to sit in on the conversation. She was good friends with Alice, and they chatted a lot in the last few weeks of Alice's life, but she won't make much sense, I'm afraid. The police have already tried."

"I'd still like to talk to her, if that's OK?" I say.

He waves me in. "I'm Aaron. Would you like a tea or coffee?"

Mrs Lupin is sitting in the large residents' lounge with a large black-and-white cat on her lap. It's definitely her, the ghost. Even sitting down with her hair in a bun, I can tell. She has the same petite body and the right silvery shade of hair. Now she's wearing grey wool trousers and a thick darker grey polo-neck jumper. Her feet are in beige fleecy indoor slipper-boots. But her face is calm and surprisingly beautiful for an old person.

She smiles when I'm brought over to her. "Hello," she says. "I won't get up. My feet hurt, but I've had them bandaged."

I shake her hand and introduce myself. I tell her I'm staying in Alice Billings's house and she says, "I know, my lovely. I'm nearly ninety."

We sit, the three of us, in a little circle. Aaron tells me that Mrs Lupin used to be a midwife and delivered babies all over the world for a charitable organization. "I love babies," she nods. "And cats."

I ask if she remembers Alice Billings, and she says, "I think she was a cat, wasn't she?"

Aaron taps a pen against his arm as if it's a drumstick.

"Er, actually Alice was a resident here," I say. "I think you might have known her. Her sister Rose was buried in the garden of the house where I'm staying."

"Oh, I remember. The dead baby," says Mrs Lupin.

I nod. I wonder how much effort the police put into interviewing her, because she seems to know a bit about what happened. "Rose was pregnant when she died."

Aaron stops tapping. "Oh yes, I saw the newspaper headline," he says.

"I looked out of my bedroom window this morning and I saw you in the garden," I say.

Mrs Lupin nods, "That's right, dear. I hope I said hello to you."

"You didn't see me," I say. "But I wondered why you'd gone there."

Mrs Lupin looks at Aaron for help.

"Can you remember why you were in Alice Billings's garden?" he asks.

"I wanted to help the girl, but I couldn't find her," she says. She whispers, "She was only sixteen. Alice is very upset about it. She told me the other day." She looks at Aaron. "Did she tell you that?"

"Alice's sister Rose died," says Aaron gently.

"It was that man's fault," says Mrs Lupin.

"Which man?" I ask, leaning forwards.

Mrs Lupin frowns. "I'm sorry. I don't remember his name..."

"Could it be Doug? Doug Billings?"

"Doug? I can't remember. That happens these days, I'm afraid."

I lean back with disappointment.

"Have I had breakfast?" she asks.

"I think so," I say, and Aaron nods.

"Well, thank you for talking to me," I say. The lounge is big. There's a man doing a crossword and another lady watering some plants on the windowsill, moving along super-slowly with a metal frame with wheels.

"It was lovely of you to visit," beams Mrs Lupin. "Were you a friend of Rose's?"

"No," I say. *I was born several decades after she died.*

Mrs Lupin strokes the cat. "Do tell Alice it wasn't her fault. I've seen babies bring joy and I've seen babies bring sorrow." She gazes at me with pale watery eyes.

I nod and glance at Aaron, but he's gesticulating something to a colleague who's in the doorway.

She strokes the cat under the chin and it purrs so loudly we both smile. "A policewoman came to see me and I told her about the dragon. She was very interested because she hadn't heard about the dragon before."

"The stone dragon?" I say. "The one in her garden?"

Mrs Lupin looks confused. "I'm not sure how many dragons there are. I'm talking about Alice's dragon. He brought her luck in the end, didn't he? Struck him down dead."

"Who was struck down dead?" I ask.

"*He* was," says Mrs Lupin with exasperation. "He deserved it." She leans her face down towards the cat. "That's what we think, anyway, isn't that right, Pippin?"

"Do you mean Doug Billings?"

She squints at me, trying to work out what I've just said. "Doug? Does he live here?"

I try one last thing. "Why didn't Alice tell the police?"

Mrs Lupin says, "I told her to tell the police. She says she's going to. She didn't say anything at first because she didn't want to wake the dog."

"The dog?"

"Let sleeping dogs lie. I think she was scared of the dog and after the dragon got him, she was happy with her baby."

Aaron rejoins the conversation, saying, "Ah, we're back to the dogs and the dragons."

Mrs Lupin says yes and she wants him to know that someone called Mrs Talbot is a pain in the arse.

Aaron laughs. "I'll have a word with her." He explains to me, "Mrs Talbot plays the radio very loudly in her room. And she prefers it when the radio isn't tuned in."

Mrs Lupin mutters, "She's a terrible menace to society."

"I'll see Leah out now, Mrs L."

"Right you are, Aaron. I won't get up – my feet hurt," says Mrs Lupin. "Bye, dear. Drive carefully and don't let the bedbugs bite."

TWENTY-EIGHT

Tatum is standing by the back door when I walk back into Roeshot House.

"Hey!" I place my hand on my heart. "You made me jump."

She doesn't smile. "Why did you go to Silverways without me? You should have waited for me."

"You were busy making the newspaper article sound like a ghost story with Poppy," I say. "And it was easier me going on my own. Less intimidating."

"What did you find out?"

"Let me have a drink of water first," I say, moving past her to the cupboard where the glasses are kept.

"Evan came round," says Tatum, as I run the tap. "It's

a shame you weren't here. He said he *might* get a chance to come back later."

I wish I hadn't gone out now. I've probably blown saying goodbye to him. "Where's he this morning?"

Ivy comes into the kitchen carrying a holdall bag. I think it belongs to Auntie Gabs. She's overheard our conversation; she says, "Evan has to go do some repairs on another property. It's turnaround day – their busiest day. He said he hopes to see you later." She dumps the holdall by the back door. "I've packed most of Mum's things. She's going to stay in bed until it's time to go."

I sag against the fridge. "I'm so annoyed I missed him."

"Tell us about Silverways," says Tatum. She's less aggressive now. "I'm not filming you, just asking." She sits at the table, legs crossed, a focused expression – like a teacher who's suddenly giving you one-hundred-per-cent attention.

"Did you find your ghost?" asks Ivy.

I nod. "Yes. Her name is Mrs Lupin. She knew Alice. She was very confused but she said she'd come to the grave to help Rose. She used to deliver babies, so I think that was the link in her head. She said what happened wasn't Alice's fault. She kept saying it was *his* fault – definitely a male, but she couldn't remember a name. And then she told me that the dragon had brought Alice luck in the end by striking him dead."

"The dragon we saw?" asks Ivy.

"I guess so," I say.

"Literally striking?" asks Ivy. "As in, Alice hit the man with the dragon?"

"Alice's husband died not long after Rose, but he had a heart attack," says Tatum. "I don't suppose Alice could crush her husband and then pretend it was a heart attack."

"No," I say. "That would be impossible."

"So you didn't get the impression that Alice had anything to do with Rose's death?" asks Ivy.

I shake my head. "It was more that she knew what had happened and did nothing. Why didn't she explain everything before she died?"

"Perhaps she thought she had more time," says Tatum. "She should have filmed an explanation, or written it down. But it's been fun trying to unravel it."

"Hmm." I'm not sure in the end how much fun it's been. "I'm going upstairs to pack my things," I say.

Tatum says she'll go to the attic and film a segment about my trip to Silverways. "By the way," she says, as she leaves the kitchen. "Have either of you noticed the grooves in the window seat up there?"

"Of course," I say.

"I have a theory they were made by fingernails. By someone holding on as best they could," says Tatum. She mimes leaning backwards on the seat and scraping the wood. "They fit my fingernails perfectly."

"Maybe," I say. The idea sounds far-fetched, but no doubt it will have a big place in her documentary.

"Either of you want to come and try it out with me? I don't mind who does the filming."

Ivy shakes her head.

"Like I said, I've got packing to do," I say. "Unless, Ivy, you want me to be with Poppy for a bit?"

"She's OK, thanks. Watching TV and slurping a milkshake," says Ivy. "The usual."

"I'm going to go into the woods later," says Tatum. "I need some long shots of the back of the house. I'd also like to pose some questions about why Rose's body wasn't buried in the woods."

"Because the Billings didn't own that land," says Ivy impatiently. "It's obvious."

"I know," snaps Tatum, "but it'll look good visually. Come and join me if you change your minds. I'll let you say some closing thoughts about the case."

"Thanks but no thanks. I'm done," I say. "I have to pack."

"Same here," says Ivy.

The bedroom is a mess and Tatum hasn't packed either. I sweep my clothes off the floor and deposit them in my suitcase, pulling out an unfamiliar black top from my bundle that must be Tatum's. I open her kitbag to chuck it in, and see a black leather strap curled up against a white T-shirt. I recognize that strap. The leather is slightly cracked along one edge. I tug. It's attached to something heavy. I push aside the clothes and see the leather case.

Binoculars. *Steve's binoculars are in Tatum's bag.*

My chest tightens as I lift them out, and blood pounds in my ears.

Tatum can't possibly want them for herself. Has she taken them purely to make the prediction about something precious being lost look as if it's come true? Was she planning on having them "turn up" at the last minute, or would she have gone home with them? Anger balloons inside me, for making fools of us and perhaps a tiny bit on Steve's behalf.

There's another explanation – somebody else has planted them in her bag for a joke, but I've seen Tatum take clothes out of there all holiday, so she would have seen the strap for sure, and it's not the sort of joke Amigos would play. I take her bag and tip it upside down on my bed, searching for anything else she's been hiding. I make sure every last thing is out of the bag by shaking it and running my hand along the bottom. A folded piece of paper falls out. I open it and it's a printout of a very short online article. The headline is *Body of Teenager Discovered Nearly 60 years After her Death*. There is no printer at Roeshot House. Tatum must have brought it with her.

I sit on her bed and rifle through her clothes in case I missed anything. I did – hidden in a sock, inside another sock, is a packet of dried rose petals.

TWENTY-NINE

I find Ivy on her knees in the little lounge, deflating Poppy's airbed.

"Look!" I hold up the binoculars and wait for her to register what they are. "I found them in Tatum's bag."

Ivy lets go of the bed and it falls away from her arms. "That's mad. That's the stupidest thing."

I hand her the article and the rose petals. "She had these in her bag too. She obviously knew about Rose's death before she came here. She'd printed this to bring with her."

I sit on the sofa, the binoculars heavy on my lap as Ivy scans the article and sniffs the petals.

"What a bitch!" says Ivy. "She totally used my family. And us Amigos."

I nod. "We were so nice to her too. She came here knowing about this, imagining how we would react on camera."

"If we'd been aware a body had been dug up in the garden, we probably wouldn't have come," says Ivy. She perches next to me on the sofa. "We gave Tatum everything she wanted – a way of getting to meet Donna and Margery and all our reactions... The predictions were a gift for her. We should never have told her about them."

I wind the strap of the binoculars round my forefinger and watch it go red before unwinding it. "I bet Tatum pushed Jakob down the stairs because of the predictions," I say. "She might even have dislodged the iron bar, just to make us think this place is haunted. That's assault! Attempted murder – one of us could have died! It's serious." I bite my lip. "I think we should tell your mum..."

Ivy places the article and petals on the floor and sinks her head into the palms of her hands, before lifting it and saying, "I should have said so before, but Mum takes more pills than she should. She does it to sleep, when things get too much."

"We have to wake her up," I say. "She needs to know. We can't wait until Mum and Steve get back. They could be ages if Steve's driving, and the roads are snowy."

"OK," nods Ivy. I gather up the binoculars, article and petals and she leads the way to her mum's bedroom in the adults' part of the house. Their landing is wider than ours, with room for a chest of drawers. Auntie Gabs's door is closed. I can picture the inside of the room from when we were little and used to run in and out of our parents' rooms in the mornings. It's large with wooden floors that gave us splinters, long faded curtains, and a big wooden bed with a headboard and footboard. My uncle once told us it was called a sleigh bed, and for a while we used it for lots of Christmas-themed role plays.

Ivy knocks on the door, lightly at first, frowning. There's no response.

I knock next, with more urgency, the sound ringing out into the landing. "Shall we go in?" I say.

Ivy's lips seem to disappear as she thinks.

"We have to," I say. I turn the handle slowly and push the door inwards. It's dark, the curtains overlapping in the middle. The room smells of body odour and stale air. "Auntie Gabs?" I call.

She has her back to us, facing towards the curtains on the far side of the bed, breathing noisily as if she has a cold. There's still no response when I call her name again more loudly. I look at Ivy, worried.

"We'll have to try later," says Ivy, turning away. "She's like this sometimes." She beckons me out of the room and I follow, pulling the door behind me until it clicks. "Tatum's up in the attic, isn't she?" she says.

I nod. "You think we should go and confront her? I don't."

Ivy shakes her head briefly, and says, "No, but I need to keep Poppy away from her. I don't trust her. She's probably got something planned for a big finale."

We look at each other. "You think she'd hurt her?" I whisper.

"She'd do anything for her film," Ivy says.

"Tell Poppy she has to be with one of us until Mum and Steve get back. She's done her bit today anyway, reading out that article," I say. "Bring her into the little lounge... I'll meet you there and help you pack up Poppy's things."

Ivy runs on ahead to the main lounge to fetch Poppy. In the little lounge, I glance again at the article. It's from an obscure online news website. I wonder what came first – Tatum finding the article and realizing she had a connection to the house through her mum, or if her mum suggested coming to Roeshot and Tatum researched the area and found the article.

I place the printout with the petals and binoculars on a coffee table where I can see them, and ram the airbed into its bag. Poppy's pile of things that was next to it looks like an abandoned island in the sea of blue carpet. It's mostly made up of her art projects, including the paper-doll people. I pick up the one that was supposed to be me, with the stuck-on skirt. She's given it chickenpox. I almost laugh out loud when I see "Steve" – he has a moustache and is wearing a bikini top and bottom. Auntie Gabs has been given rotten teeth, Mum's eyes have become two enormous love hearts, Marc and Elaine's outfits have turned black, and Tatum has a bleeding scar on her forehead. Her own paper-doll person has a twisty, climbing plant tattoo drawn all over. I pick up the Ivy one – she hasn't been touched. There's one more left: Jakob. Half of Jakob. He has an arm and leg missing.

"Leah!" Ivy's voice is far away but urgent.

I put the paper-doll people down.

"Leah – Poppy's gone!" screams Ivy.

I run into the hall as she flies towards me. "I've looked all over for her. She's gone. And so has Tatum."

She's so agitated she can't stand still; one of her knees is going back and forth like crazy. "Tatum's taken her to the woods. I know she has. Why did Poppy go with her? She must have forced her. We've got to find her."

I run to keep up with her – she's heading for the kitchen and the back door. "They can't have been gone long," I say. "Tatum was filming in the attic a few moments ago. Why didn't we hear them leave?"

Ivy turns round, doing up the three big buttons of her coat already. "Tatum must have sneaked out with her. Poppy knows she can't just leave the house without telling Mum or me, so Tatum must have lied and told her I was OK with it. See this?" She unpegs Poppy's furry-hooded coat from the hook by the door. "Poppy didn't even take her coat. What's Tatum playing at? It's minus something out there and Poppy gets cold more easily than other people."

That's a bad sign, and I know my face is only

confirming Ivy's worries. I thrust my arms into my own coat and as Ivy opens the door, I clasp it round me. There's no time to do it up because she's gone, down the side passage into the back garden. "I think they'll have gone this way," she calls.

Ivy shouts Poppy's name with increasing concern. I have a flashback of the night we went looking for Baz, and my stomach twists.

In the back garden, we strain to listen, and hear something that could be voices in the distance.

In the woods.

Ivy takes off at a run, and I follow.

It's easy to step up on to the raised flowerbed at the end of the garden and climb over the waist-high stone wall. The clearing is smaller than I remember, just the size of a small room, before the trees begin, growing so close together some of their branches overlap. The air smells of earth. We stand in the muddy leafy mulch, listening, and then, finally, we hear the voices again.

"Poppy?" screams Ivy.

There's the sound of footsteps snapping brittle twigs and leaves under foot, then, "Is that Ivy?" It's Poppy's high voice. "Why's she here?"

"Poppy?" shouts Ivy again.

The two of them come into view then. Tatum's wearing a black puffa coat, the sort that scrunches up really small and fits into a little bag. She has sunglasses on her head and a clipboard in her hand. Poppy has Tatum's furry turquoise coat over her shoulders. She looks like a monster from a kids' TV show. She's holding a large piece of silvery reflective fabric attached to a frame.

"Why aren't you wearing your own coat, Poppy?" says Ivy, her voice a few pitches higher than normal. "I brought it for you."

Poppy looks back and forth between Tatum and Ivy, panicked. "Tatum said I could wear hers if I came with her. I'm helping her with lighting." She holds up the reflector.

"What are you doing here?" asks Tatum. "I thought you didn't want to be filmed." She seems angry, and I can't work out why.

"The question should be, 'What exactly are *you* doing?'" I say. "I found the article you brought here, Tatum. You knew all about Rose even before you arrived!"

Tatum looks startled for a second, caught out. . .

"Listen, Leah—"

"No, *you* listen, Tatum! You're sick. You planned that documentary long before you ever stepped foot in Roeshot House. You've been trying to get us to react to a stupid ghost story that you made up."

"I don't know what you're talking about. There's enough craziness going on here without having to invent anything else," she said, glaring at me, and Ivy in turn.

"You stole Steve's binocolars!" Ivy hisses.

"And you brought rose petals," I added. "And lied about it!"

Tatum opens her mouth a few times, as if she's changing her mind about what to say. Then eventually she shrugs and rolls her eyes. "Ah. Well. Yes, it's true, I did know about the body in the garden. When my mum mentioned the house I looked it up, of course. I mean, I still can't believe no one here knew anything about it."

"That's why you asked your mum to ask mine if you could come with us, isn't it?" says Ivy.

Tatum raises one shoulder. "I had to go somewhere, and this was a great opportunity. It had potential. So yeah, I brought the rose petals with me. I was going to use them for a title sequence but then I heard about the predictions. They were easy to find because you kept staring at the floorboard. Poppy's ghost started it, and things kept falling into place. I went with it... And yeah, maybe I borrowed Steve's binoculars for a bit, so you lot would freak out a little over it. He left them outside by the bins. They might have been taken away as rubbish and they'd have been lost anyway."

"Freak out?" I say angrily. "*So how did you think we would react when you pushed Jakob down the stairs? Was it everything you hoped for?!*" My voice breaks at the memory of Jakob's fall.

Tatum head jerks back at this. "What? You think I pushed Jakob down the stairs? You're really accusing me of that? This is ridiculous. Poppy, come on, let's go," she says, holding out her hand. "The two of them are crazy."

"Crazy?" Ivy shouts. "You're the crazy one. Poppy, get away from her. Right now."

Poppy looks between Ivy and Tatum. She stands frozen to the spot, on the brink of tears.

"Poppy, come on," Tatum says, wiggling her outstretched fingers. "Remember our talk, and all the things you told me. I said it would all be OK, and I meant it."

"What talk? What did she say?" asks Ivy, her voice strained, arms folded tightly over Poppy's coat.

My mind is whirling. What could Poppy have said? I think of her ghost sighting, the defaced paper-doll people, her strangeness... *I could stab someone else if I wanted*, she had said.

Someone in this house will die. It was Poppy's prediction.

"Poppy?" I say, cautiously. "Poppy, what did you say to Tatum?"

She's staring down at her fur-lined boots, visibly shaking. I can't tell if it's from the cold or not.

Tatum marches over and grabs Poppy's arm at the elbow, and Poppy winces in pain. "Come on, let's get a move on," Tatum says. "We're done here."

"Wait!" shouts Ivy. "Poppy, come back. It's not safe with her!"

Tatum whips her head round. "Poppy is way better off with me, Ivy. You know that."

They keep walking, into the woods, skirting round the muddier patches, and we follow.

"Poppy, stop," shouts Ivy. "I'm not leaving you alone with Tatum."

We hear Tatum say, "Ignore her. Don't let her control you."

The muscles in Ivy's face and neck tighten. "Poppy, Tatum killed Baz!"

Poppy stops in her tracks, jerking her arm away from Tatum, and turns towards her sister, her face drained of colour.

"OK," says Tatum, stooping down. "Poppy, listen to me." She takes a deep breath. "I didn't hurt Baz. She's making it up. And I didn't push Jakob down the stairs either. I swear on my life I didn't do anything to make him fall." Then she looks up at Ivy, hatred flashing in her eyes. "I felt you push me, Ivy. I thought it was an accident at first, but the more I think about it now, you wouldn't have fallen sideways."

Ivy makes a snorting noise. "Nobody believes anything you say. You're a liar; Leah and I proved it. Why would I want to push Jakob down the stairs?"

"You tell me, Ivy," says Tatum. "The window bar that fell. Where were you when that happened? I was filming. You were pretty out of breath. Was that from running up and down to the attic?" She turns to me. "Leah. You've got to believe me."

"You're twisting everything again," I reply, my heart beating faster. Her manipulation is astounding.

"I'm not listening to any more of this," says Ivy. She

steps forward and grasps Poppy's arm. "You're coming with me."

Poppy yelps in pain. There's a resigned look on her face that's only there for a second before it passes. Then she wrenches away her arm, makes herself more upright and says, "No. I don't want to."

"Of course she doesn't," says Tatum. "She told me everything, Ivy. Everything. And I recorded all of it."

Ivy's face contorts in anger. "You—"

"Ivy, don't waste your breath on her," I interrupt. "She's vile. She'll say anything and do anything. Don't let her upset you. Leave them. Mum and Steve will be back soon."

Tatum shakes her head slowly at me. "Don't you have suspicions, Leah? I'm sure Jakob did. He could see something didn't add up about Poppy and her illness. All those questions, and ideas for getting help. I reckon that's why Ivy was keen to get him out of the way. I bet he couldn't quite believe anything bad of you, though, Ivy, what with you being Amigos and everything."

"You're evil," whispers Ivy. Her cheeks are flushed and her forehead gleams with sweat. "Don't listen to her rubbish, Leah."

Tatum points her clipboard at Ivy. "Those banana milkshakes Poppy likes so much? You never let anyone else taste them. Well Baz did, after Jakob dropped one on the floor. He got pretty sick, before he got hit by that car. Or maybe there never was an accident, was there, Ivy?"

Ivy stares at Tatum, her breath heavy. Poppy drops the reflector and cowers against a tree.

"Let's take a sample of that milkshake mix," says Tatum. "Let's run some tests, shall we?"

"Tatum, why would Ivy want to hurt Poppy?" I ask. But nausea rises as my brain sifts through everything she's said. Poppy's so fragile. I think of her yelping when Tatum grabbed her. And again when Ivy grabbed her. I picture her plant tattoo winding up that arm with the big purple flower in the middle. It was an odd sort of purple. There were other colours in it. As if it wasn't drawn on. As if it was a bruise.

It's not the sort of place you knock easily, the inside of your elbow.

I think of those paper-doll people. The Ivy one was left alone. Was Poppy too scared of her to make fun of her, even in paper form?

Or was it Ivy who defaced Poppy's dolls?

"You'll regret this," says Ivy. She turns and heads back to the house.

I turn to Tatum. "You have done so much damage," I spit. I'm exhausted by it all, but Mum and Steve will sort this out, the lies and the accusations from the truth.

Tatum holds up her phone. Has she been recording this conversation? "You should see what Poppy said."

I'm aware of a strange shouting. Ivy is running back towards us. She no longer has Poppy's coat but she has something else. As she comes closer I see she's holding some kind of spade. Black metal.

She raises her arm. Words push themselves to the front of my brain. *"I thought there was an old coal shovel in the garage, but I could only find the gardening spade."* Clive said that when he came in from burying Baz. This is the old coal shovel.

I'm close enough to see there's stuff on the spade part. It's thick . . . like congealed blood with lumps . . . like bits of mashed meat.

Baz. Yelping and not comprehending. Brutal blows. Crushed face. Unimaginable pain. Pulped brain. Discarded by the bins.

I dry-heave. "Nooooooo," I half scream, half-choke as Ivy brings the shovel down on Tatum's head.

THIRTY

Tatum doesn't have a chance to fight back against the frenzied blows. As she slumps to the ground unconscious, I leap towards Poppy and take her hand.

"Run," I sob. For a panic-drenched moment I can't tell which direction the house is in, but when I do, I drag her towards it.

"I can't run," she says. Her whole body's quaking.

I pull the enormous coat off her so she can move more easily. "You can," I say. *"Run!"*

As we stumble towards the wall, she says, "You go on." Her face is screwed up with pain and fear.

We hear the sound of Ivy smashing Tatum's phone with the shovel. This can't be about destroying the documentary.

It's what Poppy told Tatum, the words which were recorded. I don't understand what's going on, but I know I'm petrified of Ivy and I have to get Poppy to safety.

I don't have time to argue with Poppy. I scoop her up like a baby, and I run through the mud, wide-legged to help me balance, my back arched too far, burning with the strain. At the garden wall, I say, "Run to the first house. Get help," and then I drop her over into the flowerbed. She lands on her feet, and steps unsteadily down on to the lawn.

I glance back and see Ivy making her way towards us. She doesn't have the shovel, but the determined look on her face is chilling.

It'll only take minutes before she catches up, but at least I'm not going to be caught off-guard like Tatum. "Run!" I scream at Poppy as I clamber over the wall.

Poppy's run is a strange sort of jog. She's terrifyingly slow and Ivy has almost caught up to us. I lift Poppy up and carry her for as long as I can before I feel Ivy tugging me backwards. "Run. Go. Please," I gasp as I'm forced to drop her.

I pivot round and punch Ivy. It makes contact but has no meaningful impact because she's gripped my arm. She doesn't look like my cousin and Amigo any more. She's a person possessed with fury. She lunges for my hair. I lift my other arm to stop her.

"Did you really do those things?" I ask, playing for time, so Poppy will make it down the driveway. Maybe someone will be passing by.

"You wouldn't understand," says Ivy. She's twisting my arm behind my back.

"Stop it, you're hurting me!" I cry. I duck down and get out of the twist, breaking free and backing away. I slip on the wet grass and Ivy gets hold of my coat.

"Yeah, well, I hurt too, Leah. And poor, poor Poppy? She hurts all the time. So she needs help. She needs me."

I have a chance to break free. My coat's not done up. All I have to do is pull one arm out then the other. Fast. Now.

First sleeve. Second sleeve. I'm free.

I sprint down the side passage. Poppy isn't even at the back door yet; there's no way she'll get down the drive. "Go inside," I shout and shove her through the door, tumbling in after her and then pressing my weight against the door to slam it shut behind us. I turn the key in the lock, pull across the bolt and breathe out.

"Leah!" Ivy is pounding on the door. "Let me speak to you. Leah!"

I back away. Think: where else could she get in? Hide Poppy, or tell her to go upstairs and wait with Auntie Gabs? I know every hiding place in this house ... but so does Ivy.

"See if you can wake your Mum," I say.

Poppy stares at me, her face almost expressionless with trauma.

"Go! Please go." I'm crying; I don't want to cry; it'll blur my vision. I race out of the kitchen, down the corridor and across the hall to the front door. It's locked, but I attach the security chain in place. I run to the conservatory and check the door, looking through the glass into the empty garden, knowing I should be calling an ambulance for Tatum in the woods beyond. If we had phone service.

No windows are open, not in this weather. Would Ivy break one to get in? After seeing what she did to Tatum, I wouldn't put it past her.

I can't hear any sounds from outside. Ivy has stopped shouting. Where's she gone?

I run upstairs to Auntie Gabs's bedroom. The door's open but I don't see Poppy.

"Auntie Gabs? Get up. Ivy's gone beserk." I rush to the other side of the bed to shake her, and see Poppy, sitting on the floor against the bed in a tiny ball, knees tucked up to her chest.

"You couldn't wake her?" I say.

Poppy shakes her head.

I pull the duvet back. Auntie Gabs is still wearing the same clothes I last saw her in, days ago, when Ivy pushed Jakob down the stairs.

She half-opens red-rubbed eyes.

"Please!" I scream near her face and she flinches.

"In a minute," she croaks and closes her eyes.

"Leave Mum to sleep."

I wheel round to see Ivy. There's a quiet smile on her face and blood on her hands.

Words fly out as my mind spirals. "How did you get in?"

"The conservatory. The door's so flimsy."

Fear pulses through me like a new heartbeat. I push Poppy with my leg, indicating for her crawl under the bed.

"Where's Poppy?"

Where are Mum and Steve? Keep Ivy away from Poppy. Distract her.

"She went out of the front to get help."

"You're lying." Ivy comes closer. There's a fake plant on the chest of drawers. A white pot and some kind of fern. I reach for it and throw it at Ivy, then run. I don't even know if it hit her, I just run.

I run on boneless legs. I stumble down the stairs, Ivy three – now two – steps behind me.

I fly past the front door, locked and chained, with no time to fumble with them. There's no choice but to keep running, through the hall, up the first set of stairs, where I glance out of the window.

Please let there be a car coming up the drive. Or Evan. Anyone.

I can hardly see through my tears. I run to my bedroom and hesitate for a split second. The door to the attic room is sturdier. It's a proper fire door. I can wedge a sofa up against it. That will buy me more time.

I fall up the last step to the door, and that costs me. When I reach it, I feel a hand grab my ankle.

"Final Amigo get-together?" she says.

There's a deadness in her eyes; I tell myself it wasn't there before. If it had been, I'd have seen it, surely?

I kick out, breaking free, and scramble out of her grasp and into the attic. I slam the door and hold my foot against it while she rattles the door handle. "Ivy, what are you doing? What's happened? We're Amigos," I plead, and my body slides down to the floor, my back to the door. I eye the room for the closest heavy object.

I hear Ivy laugh derisively. "Amigos!"

"What about Jakob? He's our friend!"

I brace myself against the door as she gives it a shove. I hear her say, "Friend? Friends don't interfere! I told him he couldn't have a milkshake. I didn't want to have to kill Baz. It really hurt me to do that, but Mum would have taken him to the vet. And then, well, then the questions would come."

I shake my head, tears flowing freely now.

"I've always known Mum prefers Poppy over me. I overheard her tell someone that she had a gush of love for Poppy as soon as she was born, and that hadn't happened with me." She sighs impatiently. "You wouldn't know what I'm talking about. You're an only child. You've become spoilt since your dad left. Always moaning. But you can see him whenever you want."

"So you tried to kill Jakob?"

"He's not dead, is he? He just fell and had to go to the hospital. He'll be fine."

There's very little saliva in my mouth but I ask, "Why didn't the doctors work it out?"

"Poppy's illness?"

I hate how she calls it an illness.

"Doctors aren't as clever as you think. I make sure she doesn't snitch. I make her think she's going mad." She pauses for a moment, then adds, "I've always had lots of ideas, haven't I, Leah?"

"Yes," I say in a low, hoarse voice. I'm listening for a door slam, footsteps on the stairs, somebody to rescue me. The door stops rattling and Ivy is quiet. I think I can hear her going back down the stairs but I can't be certain. I call her name, unsure whether it's a trap, yet worried she's gone to hunt down Poppy. I wait more minutes before standing up, keeping my foot in place against the door. I weigh up the risk of leaving the door for a second and dragging the big armchair over, the one that Ivy always sits in.

I count myself down then rush at the chair. Once it's in place, I drag over the chest of drawers as well, but I'm still panicked. I have to get help for Tatum and Poppy.

I go over to the attic window, looking out to see if there's some way I can lower myself to the ground, make a proper run for it. My fingers graze the random grooves in the window seat, the ones Tatum said fit her fingernails. I realize with a creeping dread she might be right. They aren't random. They fit the pattern of someone clinging on to the window.

The door crashes against the armchair and the chest of drawers, and to my horror they shift just enough in less than a second to let Ivy through. "Taking in the view?" she asks. "Or are you still fixating on Rose?"

I back up against the window seat, and everything seems to go into slow motion as I notice she has a large knife in her hand.

We sit within a circle of lit tea lights, holding hands. Me, Jakob and Ivy. Poppy is fast asleep on the sofa; Ivy will carry her down to their bedroom later. We knew she wouldn't last until midnight but we'd promised she could join in.

"Two predictions each," Ivy says. "We'll go around twice."

"I'll start," I say, and take a deep breath.

Jakob is trying to stifle giggling.

It needs to sound weighty, like a phrase from an old book. "Something of great value will be lost," I say, then pull my hands away to write it down on my notepad, pleased with it. "Your turn, Jakob."

Ivy crosses the room and comes right up to me, and I can't breathe. Do I try to fight her? Scream?

"I wish I didn't have to do this," she whispers in my ear, and my heart spasms. I think of the sparrowhawk Steve pointed out earlier in the week, circling for its prey. "We're family. And we've had such nice times together."

I sit rigid. If I don't move and don't speak she might talk until someone comes. Except I'm shaking uncontrollably.

"Even this time was good in parts," says Ivy. "Learning about Alice and Rose. I respect Alice. She was smart. No one suspected a thing until she told them."

"Alice didn't kill her sister," I manage to say, desperately stalling. "It was her husband." All I can think about is that knife.

"OK, OK," Jakob says. "Ommmmm..." He lifts his face to the ceiling. "Errmmmmm... Ummm..."

Ivy sighs. "Jakob! Take this seriously."

"All right. An actual ghost will be seen," he says.

"That's creepy," I whisper, as I write it down. Did I set the wrong tone with my prediction?

Ivy looks at the bookshelves. The book we were reading to each other the last couple of nights is there, face up on the edge. It has a horrible cover of twisted trees in a dark wood. "Someone in this house will be in a car accident."

We look at her.

"Sorry," she says.

We get it. The parents of the teenage siblings in that story died in a car accident.

Her hand descends quickly, grabbing my hair, and the shock and the pain gives me a strange vision of Doug Billings grabbing Rose Strathmortimer in the same way. Ivy and I are the same size, but she's stronger than me. She leans over me and I shrink away.

Somehow she manages to open the window with one hand, and cold air streams in behind me.

My second prediction is, "There will be an unexpected twist of fate". I don't even know what it means. It sounds like a riddle. I say it again as I list it as the fourth prediction.

Jakob mutters, "Nice. My prediction is, 'An Amigo will be unlucky in love their whole life.'"

I give his hand a gentle squeeze.

We hear a noise from the sofa. "Have I missed it?" Poppy is on her feet. There's a crease mark on her cheek where it was squished against the blanket. "Why didn't you wake me?" she wails. She walks up to my notebook and squints at it.

"We're on the last one," says Ivy. "That's the most special one. We saved it for you."

Poppy's face lifts.

"Take your time," says Jakob. "You can't rush a prediction."

"Yes, walk three times round the room, and come and sit in the circle and hold hands," I say.

We exchange amused glances as she walks ceremoniously round the attic.

"Concentrate, Pops," says Ivy.

She steps over the tea lights and comes to sit between Jakob and me, upright and solemn. She knows how to work a pause. "Someone in this house will die," she says slowly.

The words hover in the candlelight as we look at each other, with shock that turns to a deep sense of unease. Poppy nods before anyone has a chance to ask her if she's sure.

"You can't have that," I say.

"What have you been watching on TV?" asks Jakob.

"Is this to do with Dad?" asks Ivy.

Poppy sucks her lips inwards. Life hasn't been easy for her. "I don't know why I said it."

Ivy's pushing me towards the open window, holding the knife near my throat. I grip the edge of the window seat. Panic dissolves my thought processes. I hear my screams mixed with Rose's. She didn't want to die either. My nails dig into the grooves she made decades before me.

"Help!" I scream. "Please help me!"

I imagine Alice was at the other end of the house when Doug pushed Rose through the window. Did she help her husband bury her sister because she was scared of him?

"Nobody's coming," says Ivy. She throws the knife on the floor. "I don't need that yet." She places both hands round my neck. "You and Tatum had such a morbid fascination with the body in the garden! It's terrible how your imaginations spun out of control, and it ended in tragedy. Tatum shoved you out of the window, as if you were Rose." She's crying.

I can barely draw air into my lungs. I hit out with my arms but I can't make contact with her.

Keep fighting.

Little by little, Ivy is pushing me towards the open window, head first, but I'm on my back. It feels as if my neck might snap. I see orange and black shapes. There's a rasping noise coming out of my mouth.

"I fought Tatum. I tried to save you. I chased her to the woods. There was a knife and a shovel. We fought really hard. I was injured badly with the knife. The one on the floor. It's waiting for me." She sniffs through her tears. "I'm sorry, Leah. I'm so sorry it had to happen like this."

I'm running out of time.

I can't hold on to the window seat any more. I hear Ivy's sobs. The orange shapes have gone. There is only darkness. *Please no. I'm going to fall.*

I think of the rush of air when I've jumped off the triangulation point at Chandler's Hill, the thrill and panic of falling.

Now there's fear and nothing else. I kick one final time. A fast ballerina kick—

I'm dragged back. My head bumps over the windowsill. My throat feels constricted but I can breathe.

I smell something familiar. Aftershave. "You're safe, Leah." It's Steve.

He lifts me up and takes me to the sofa nearest the window. I know that because it's lumpy underneath my back. I recognize the shape of those lumps.

"Please, Leah, open your eyes," he says. "I knew something was wrong, but I didn't know what. We shouldn't have left you here. I'm sorry."

I want to say thank you. And sorry.

Mum's voice next.

Evan's voice.

Sirens.

It's over.

I open my eyes.

THIRTY-ONE

At first I said I'd never go back to Roeshot House, but when Evan got in touch to say he hoped I could be there when the birdhouse went up in June, I reconsidered. I said he should invite Jakob and possibly Tatum, but in the end neither could come – Jakob because he was playing his violin in a concert, his arm finally healed, and Tatum because her parents wouldn't let her come anywhere near Pinhurst or our families again.

Evan says he's picked June because the roses up the side of the garage will be flowering, and as soon as we turn into the driveway I see them. They're dramatic reds and pinks, and masses of them. It's odd being here in summertime: half the house is in full sun, the other in shade, and the garden is noisy with birds and insects.

There are eight of us: Mum, Steve and me, Evan, Clive, Evan's mum and sister Lily, and Margery. Evan and I hug, and it's nowhere near as awkward as I thought it would be, and I say polite hellos to the others. We stand next to each other for the odd little ceremony. Clive says a few words about remembering a sixteen-year-old who'd had her life cut short. Evan steps forward to hang the birdhouse on to a hook and we clap, which feels appropriate and cheesy at the same time. He's painted the name *Rose* up the side farthest away from the house so it's kind of private. Margery says there's going to be a proper headstone in the Pinhurst graveyard for her, but I reckon the birdhouse wins, hands down, as a memorial.

Afterwards we walk to the back of the house, passing the place where Rose most likely fell, and where I almost did. Steve places his arm round my shoulder as I look up at the attic window. I don't shrug him off. I catch the faint smell of aftershave and it makes me feel safe.

Clive says there's toughened glass up there now and the new window doesn't open. This day isn't about Ivy, but I can't help thinking of her in the secure unit.

We play croquet on the patch of immaculate lawn in front of the conservatory with the set Margery bought for the house. She makes sure we stick to the rules, and the game gets fierce. I want to remember this scene: an odd mix of people in the sunshine, laughing, and the satisfying tap of a mallet against a ball.

Mum wins. She's quite a competitive person on the quiet.

We go back to Evan's house for lunch, and after we've eaten, he and I go to his workshop and I see the most recent birds he's carved. Evan's started selling them in the gift shop in Riddingham for crazy-stupid prices. I've arranged to buy one at mates' rates to give to Steve for his birthday.

I tell Evan that Steve hasn't shed his annoying habits, but he's all right when you get to know him properly, and Mum thinks he's the greatest.

Evan wraps the plump little sedge warbler up in tissue paper, then gives me a wooden heart he's made. It fits nicely into my hand, like a pebble. I'm glad I had my first kiss with him. He was there for me on Skype when I needed him as I tried to process what had happened, but I recognize our thing was never going to be long-term. He's going out with someone from the village now, and she sounds nice.

I doubt I'll ever come back to Pinhurst. Sofia says I have to go to a party with her at New Year. She's still going out with Dan, but it's gone down a few notches, so we're back to sitting on the sea wall a lot.

Not long after I've come back from Pinhurst for the birdhouse ceremony, Evan messages to tell me about a photo his dad found lodged behind the chest of drawers in my bedroom at Roeshot House. He sends the image through: it's of Doug with Alice and Rose, posing at an event in evening outfits, only they're not ready for the shot. Alice is talking to someone you can't see, and because Rose is side-on to the camera, you can see Doug's hand on her bottom, pushing her towards him so her chest is up against him. He's laughing; Rose isn't. I forward it to Jakob, and say I bet we were right to think the stone dragon finally brought Alice luck when Doug was struck down dead. Jakob replies with exuberant shock-face emojis and a meme of a dragon looking very pleased with itself. We send it on to a journalist in Riddingham who's been writing stories about the case.

We're much more in touch, me and Jakob. Most days we check in with each other to see how life is puttering along and, occasionally, what atrocities our parents have committed. The Amigo days are over, but Jakob and I will always be friends. We don't know much about what's going on with Tatum. We know from the police investigation that she's recovering still, and a month ago she started posting film clips on Instagram, so we hope she's OK.

Among other things, Ivy was diagnosed with fabricated or induced illness (FII), also known as Munchausen's syndrome by proxy. She liked the attention of Poppy being ill. Auntie Gabs's spiralling dependence on medication made it easy for Ivy to take on the role of her sister's kind and dedicated carer. Pesticide was discovered in Poppy's banana milkshake powder. Ivy confessed she would switch to an uncontaminated mix during days leading up to any blood tests.

Poppy's slowly getting better, but her psychiatrist says the psychological effects will be with her for a long time. They have a social worker now, while Auntie Gabs is getting back on her feet and coming to terms with everything, and Poppy's granny on her dad's side has moved in with them.

Last week Poppy came to stay with Mum and me for a few days and was noisier than I've ever known her, and much more healthy-looking. Her favourite thing was sitting on the sea wall with a bag of chips.

She asked if Steve is going to move in with us, and I said, "Who knows?"

But not in an angry way.

ACKNOWLEDGEMENTS

Linas Alsenas, my fantastic and supportive editor, I couldn't have done this without you, thank you. Eishar Brar, thank you too for your always-helpful comments.

Thanks to Sean Williams for creating another creepy cover that fits so well with the others. Olivia Horrox, you are a brilliant publicist, and being at Hay Festival with you and Sarah Lough last year was a real highlight. Thanks to the rest of the talented Scholastic team.

Becky Bagnell, my agent, thank you for continued help and friendship.

Thank you to Jakob Asp who won a bid to be a character in *Your Turn to Die* in aid of Authors for Grenfell, and to Donna David and her daughter Sofia who were outbid at the last moment but donated anyway.

A special mention to students at Esher High School, especially those who hang out in the library even when it's not raining. Thank you to Barbara Smith for her in-house promotion of my books, and to the awesome library monitors.

Many thanks to the book bloggers and booktubers who've reviewed my books, and to readers who've taken the trouble to contact me. Hello to Kian!

Thank you to lovely friends who've kept me bouncing along this year, and my family whose support never wavers.

To my daughters Phoebe, Maia and Sophie, you make me proud. Thanks for the chats and laughs, and for answering my strange questions.

Also by Sue Wallman:

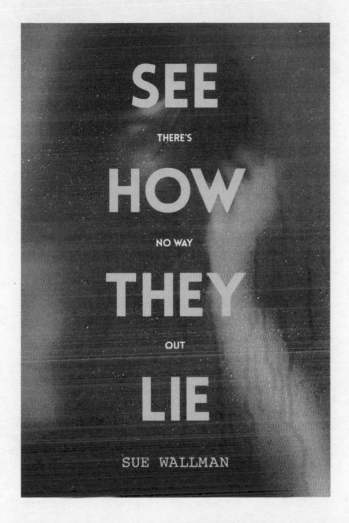

Mae believes she's lived all her life in Hummingbird
Creek, an elite wellness retreat, because her father is a
psychiatrist there. But when Mae breaks the rules, the
response is severe. She starts questioning everything, and
at the Creek, asking questions can be dangerous.

lying

you can't

about

hide the truth

last

forever

summer

SUE WALLMAN

Skye is looking for an escape. Her sister died in a tragic accident and her parents think a camp for grieving teens might help her. But when she arrives, Skye starts receiving text messages from someone pretending to be her dead sister. Skye knows it's time to confront the past. But what if the danger is right in front of her?